About the Author

Kurt Odenwald is a native of New York. He completed undergraduate studies in communication and journalism, and graduate studies in film and television. He has worked in academia for many years and has professional experience in the United States, United Kingdom, Latin America, and Asia. He currently resides in New England.

Shades of Darkness

Kurt Odenwald

Shades of Darkness

Olympia Publishers
London

www.olympiapublishers.com
OLYMPIA PAPERBACK EDITION

A CIP catalogue record for this title is
available from the British Library.

ISBN: 978-1-80074-638-1

This is a work of fiction.
Names, characters, places and incidents originate from the writer's
imagination. Any resemblance to actual persons, living or dead, is
purely coincidental.

First Published in 2023

Olympia Publishers
Tallis House
2 Tallis Street
London
EC4Y 0AB

Printed in Great Britain

Dedication

This book is dedicated to: My mother, Leonor, whose wisdom and strength provided the foundation of my character; my sister, Karla, whose intelligence and guidance helped me forge a path in life; and the memory of my father, Carlos, who will always be an important part of me.

Contents

Dixie Cups

Tyler stared at his reflection in the bathroom mirror and tried to smile. He could not do it. There were dark circles under his bloodshot eyes; his skin had taken on a sickly, yellow pallor, and was beginning to sag. His nicotine-stained teeth contrasted sharply with a week's worth of beard growth, speckled with unruly whiskers of gray. It was truly a lamentable sight.

There was no reason to smile anyway, so why even bother trying? His wife had died three years ago, and his two grown children wanted nothing to do with him. He had been a brave soldier, a successful business owner, a loyal husband, and a loving father, and all for what? He was now reduced to a pathetic shell of a human being, living in a deplorable tenement in the South Bronx. Where had it all gone wrong? Tyler did not know. Tyler did not remember. Tyler did not care.

Today was as good a day as any to go through with it. He had been saying the same thing over and over to himself for the past two weeks, but today he really *would* do it. Of course, that had also been his intention since the idea first materialized in his head. Just do it. Stop contemplating it so much, and just take the step. It will all be over in a matter of seconds, so enough philosophizing and cheap psychobabble, and just get it over with.

Tyler splashed freezing water on his face as if to fill himself with resolve. He exited the bathroom and took confident steps toward his footlocker, which was a relic from his military days. Without hesitation, he opened it and stared at the solution to all his problems. There was something poetic about the moment. It was December 31st. The last day of the year. It would be quick and efficient, and then there would be nothing. No pain. No suffering. No remorse. Nothing. Why begin another year of the same? Just wipe the slate clean and let others worry about the future. The moment was now, and the timing could not be more perfect.

Ready to take the definitive step, Tyler was startled out of his reverie by the sound of loud banging in the corridor and the sound of choking sobs. Annoyed at being interrupted at such a sublime moment, Tyler stepped out into the corridor yelling, "What the fuck?"

The noise was not the issue. Pounding and screaming was an everyday affair in the South Bronx tenement, and Tyler had pretty much learned to ignore it, but there was something different in the sound of these cries. There was true desperation in them. The hopelessness came across as loudly as the volume itself.

Tyler spotted the source of the commotion at the end of the hall. A small, elderly woman with unkempt strands of thin, gray hair sporting a ratty, pastel house dress was wailing at the top of her lungs and hitting a neighbor's door with as much strength as her fragile, bony hands permitted. Tyler walked up to her angrily. "What's the problem, lady? Are you hurt?"

The old lady was momentarily startled by Tyler's massive frame, but turned to him nonetheless, and started blubbering incoherently as giant tears rolled down the deep canals of her heavily wrinkled face. Tyler said, "I don't understand what you're saying. Do you need me to call someone?"

This seemed to upset the old woman even more, and she started shrieking and crying even harder than before. This was too much for Tyler as he mercilessly yelled at her, "Stop screaming, you old bag! What's the problem, already?"

The harsh tone and loud volume of Tyler's voice seemed to stun her into silence as she sniffled like a recently scolded five-year-old, and held up an old paper cup, yellowed by use with the bottom torn out due to moisture.

"My Dixie cup ripped. How am I supposed to take my medicine now?" Tyler stared at her incredulously. All this fuss over a fucking Dixie cup? You have got to be kidding. And whose door was she trying to knock down anyway? Maybe she had locked herself out of her own apartment. It did not really matter, though. He just wanted her to stop crying.

"Wait here," Tyler said in a commanding voice.

The old woman simply nodded dumbly.

Tyler rushed back to his apartment, went through his kitchen cabinets, and grabbed half a dozen plastic cups. He rushed back to her and placed them in the old lady's hands.

"There," he said simply.

The old lady stared at the cups as if not understanding and said, "These aren't Dixie cups, and they aren't white. I like the ones with the little flowers on them."

Tyler stared at her in disbelief and did not know what to say. He did not know whether they were Dixie cups or not. Did they even *make* Dixie cups anymore? Tyler did not know, but he felt he had to say something.

"They're the newest line. The colors are supposed to match your décor."

As the old woman squinted at him suspiciously, Tyler continued. "They're stronger, last longer and are better for the environment too," he added, embarrassed at his awkwardly delivered and utterly ridiculous impromptu advertising campaign.

"OK," the old woman answered simply.

Apparently, she had been sold on the concept.

"You can take me home now," she ordered, pointing to a half-open door across the hall.

Tyler escorted his neighbor to her apartment, but before he could take his leave, she hugged him with surprising strength for such a frail-looking woman.

"You're such a nice boy. Come by and see me later. We'll have milk and cookies."

Tyler felt his heart melt inside his chest and hugged her back as enormous tears rolled down his weather-beaten face. He would have to change his plans. He was looking forward to having milk and cookies with his new friend.

Fantasy

Last night had been the final straw for Vinny. He was not going to continue wasting his life away looking for something that was obviously never going to come. Perhaps it was for the best. Some people were just meant to be alone. His mother had accepted it. She had become a widow at thirty, and never remarried. Suitors had come and gone, some more insistent than others, to woo the beautiful young widow, and audition for the role of Vinny's new father. She had never even given them the slightest chance. She was a devout Catholic who refused to let go of the memory of her late husband, and for twenty years dedicated her entire existence to Vinny, losing both her looks, and any previous trace of individuality she had once possessed in the process.

Of course, Vinny did not share his mother's religious fervor. He could not fathom the idea of twenty sexless years. He was not exactly what one would call an experienced young man, but he was by no means a virgin. At twenty-four he had had four sexual partners. The first, the prostitute that had taken his virginity, the second, his first and only love, and the final two, highly unsuccessful attempts at trying to simultaneously remember and forget the second one.

Today was Vinny's twenty-fifth birthday. He had planned on completing his quarter of a century on the planet with a girlfriend, but last night had not gone at all as he had expected. He had been seeing Melissa for the past six months. Seeing was a very loose term, considering he had not so much as kissed her on the lips, but he had been willing to wait. This was true love, and Melissa was worth the wait, or so he had thought.

They had met at an Internet café in Manhattan. They had been in the same chat room for about thirty minutes before realizing they were sitting right next to each other. It was a Tolkien fan chat room, and when they introduced themselves in person, they connected on so many levels that it was unreal. They were both into fantasy literature and agreed that escapism through this medium was therapeutic rather than harmful. They both loved classic rock, although there was a clear difference between them when it came to crowning The Beatles or The Rolling Stones kings. It was amazing. It was perfect. It was too good to be true, and as a matter of fact, it was. Melissa had a boyfriend and though she did not mention it until almost three weeks later, Vinny had sensed it from the start. He pretended not to care when she finally brought it up, but did a very poor job of concealing his disappointment.

He told Melissa how he felt, but accepted a friendship with her, nonetheless. She had been in her current relationship since high school, and was apparently not ready to call it off, but also told him that only time would tell. This was all Vinny needed to hear. He fell head over heels in love with her and, truth be told, she appeared to have the same feelings toward him. Although they were not officially a couple, Vinny and Melissa were always together. Their embraces were intense, and not particularly fraternal. Their friendly kisses on the cheek were a bit too close to the lips without ever actually entering the forbidden territory. When they looked at each other, there was so much longing and desire that anyone would think that they had just made love and were now in the process of initiating foreplay once again. In short, for all practical purposes, Vinny and Melissa were the perfect couple except for the fact that they were not.

Vinny often wondered what Melissa's boyfriend thought about all the time she spent with Vinny, but he never asked her. That was a taboo subject. Although they never talked about it, it was always there, hovering incessantly over their would-be romance. It was never a topic of discussion between them, but every time they said good night, it was there in its full splendor, wordlessly haunting them, and shattering any possibility of them being together.

Vinny suffered in silence for six, long months and finally made a decision. He would confront Melissa about their relationship, and they would both declare their undying love for one another and live happily ever after. Love conquers all, after all, doesn't it?

They met on a Friday night to celebrate the eve of Vinny's birthday. After an expensive and undeniably romantic dinner, paid in full by a credit card Melissa produced from her purse, successfully covering the cardholder's name, they went to the pier to watch the sunset together.

"Happy birthday, Vinny," she said and gave him one of her characteristically long, close-to-the-lips kisses on the cheek. "Aren't sunsets beautiful?"

"You're beautiful," Vinny said and stared deeply into her eyes.

Melissa looked down demurely, and then looked up with huge, long-lashed eyes. *There will not be a more perfect time than this*, Vinny thought, and went for it. He hooked his right arm around her waist and pulled her roughly toward him. She barely had enough time to gasp before he was kissing her deeply. He felt her tense at first and then relax, surrendering herself completely to the moment. They kissed each other hungrily, and then suddenly, without any kind of warning, she pulled away from him, and slapped him hard across the face.

There are many times in life when words can simply not express what one is thinking or feeling. This was one of those times for Vinny. He had no idea what to think or feel, and even less of an idea of what he should do. He simply stared at Melissa dumbfounded. She took a couple of steps back from him.

"Vinny, what are you doing? You and I are just friends."

The final two words made Vinny's blood begin to boil. What was it about women and their ridiculous *just friends* concept? Did they not understand that this was the absolute worst possible thing you could say to a man? I do not like you. I hate you. You disgust me. I would rather chew off my own limbs than go out with you. Any one of these colorful phrases was more humane compared to the *just friends* let down. But Melissa had just used the most horrid one of all, and the worst thing was that she had done it immediately after, what ten seconds ago, his brain had registered as the best kiss of his life. *And* she had slapped him. Nobody had ever slapped him. Growing up as an Italian American in New Jersey, this was quite unprecedented. This woman, who had practically been his girlfriend for the past six months, and who had undoubtedly, thoroughly enjoyed the kiss they had just shared, had just slapped him, and pulled the *just friends* card to add insult to injury.

While all this was going through Vinny's mind, Melissa shifted uncomfortably from one foot to another, looking everywhere except at Vinny's face.

"I mean … where is this coming from, Vinny?"

Where is this coming from? Had he heard correctly? Was she *that* clueless, or just brazen to be asking him such a question after six months of spending the better part of every day together?

The *just friends* comment now totally forgotten; Vinny's temple began throbbing with Melissa's ridiculous question. Where is this coming from? Where the hell did she *think* it was coming from?

Vinny's previous inability to form words was now completely cured. What came out was a blasphemous rosary of curses that would have cost him a mouthful of soap had his mother been in the vicinity.

"Where is this coming from? Where the fuck do you *think* it's coming from?" he roared. "Or were you just planning to string me along by the cock forever?"

Melissa wrinkled her face in disgust.

"Your Jersey guinea is showing, Vincent," she said steadily.

"Fuck you!" he spat out.

He was on a roll and was not about to stop now.

"You are the biggest fucking cockteaser I have ever met in my entire life! How does your sponsor..." Vinny paused for dramatic effect. "Oh, excuse me, I mean your boyfriend, put up with the two-timing likes of you?"

"I have never been unfaithful to Devon," she answered defensively. She was already on the verge of tears.

This was not going well. And now, on top of everything else, he knew the prick's name. And, of course, it could not be Bill or Tom, which he could easily have identified with a blue-collar man like himself. It had to be Devon. It sounded like a wealthy aristocrat who belonged on an episode of *Dynasty* or *Falcon Crest*. No, this was not going well at all. Vinny had played out this scene repeatedly in his head, and this was not even remotely close to what was supposed to happen. Melissa was supposed to realize that she really loved Vinny, break it off with the previously anonymous, sophisticated boyfriend, and live happily ever after with Vinny Di Nuzzo from Jersey City.

At that moment, Vinny made another decision. In a very calm voice, filled more with resignation than disappointment, he looked directly at Melissa.

"You know what? I give up."

And with these words Vinny turned, and walked away, leaving Melissa standing alone at the pier staring at him with a comical expression of surprise and confusion on her face.

This entire fiasco had happened less than twelve hours ago, but now Vinny was a new man. He was turning twenty-five today, and this would mark the beginning of his new life. He looked at himself in the bathroom mirror and saw the shadow of stubble beginning to form on his face. He picked up a razor and then decided against it. He would give the scruffy look a try. He looked around his studio apartment and smiled. It was extremely neat for a bachelor living on his own. Everything was clean, and in its place. The only hint of a mess was a couple of plates in the kitchenette sink, and his unmade bed, two things which he refused to tend to on the weekends unless he had company, which was not very often. It was a nice little space.

When he had first moved to New York four years ago, he had wanted to get a place in Manhattan, but rent prices were sky high, and he had no intention a sharing a loft with a dozen other people just so he could say he lived in Tribeca or the Village. He had been quite lucky to find this studio in Brooklyn for a reasonable price before it had started to become trendy a couple of years ago. Of course, trendy only meant that Manhattanites that could no longer afford to live on the island had to move, thus magically giving certain areas of Brooklyn the status of trendy.

Vinny went through a light workout routine that consisted of basic stretching and form exercises. He was in good shape without looking like a magazine model. He was tall, trim and had a well-proportioned physique. He had thick, black hair, olive skin and green eyes. In fact, Vinny was an extremely attractive man by most standards. His lack of success with the fairer sex was not due to his looks. His inability to connect with them was the issue at hand. He was an utter failure at approaching women, or, as his friends were fond of saying to him, he had no game. Women would frequently confuse his extreme shyness with arrogance and, oddly enough, seem disappointed when they realized he was not arrogant at all. The other serious problem that Vinny had was that he was a hopeless romantic.

There are many people who describe themselves as hopeless romantics, but in Vinny's case, it was truly hopeless. If a pretty girl smiled at him on the subway, he was already picking out baby names for their future children, an activity that proved to be quite futile considering that nine out of ten times he could not even work up the nerve to smile back. The relationships he *had* had were because the women had approached *him,* and practically offered themselves to him on a silver platter.

It was noon by the time he finished his routine. After showering and a light lunch, he went to his videotape library to choose a movie. What immediately caught his eye was the cartoon version of 'The Lord of the Rings.' This made him think of Melissa and he cursed aloud when he began to feel his eyes getting wet.

"You don't deserve my tears, bitch!"

He took out the trilogy, lay down on his bed and started watching. It was an incredibly sophisticated animation considering that it had been produced in the seventies. He did not care much for the way it had been divided, though. The first movie was called 'The Hobbit.' The second one was called 'The Lord of the Rings' and covered 'The Fellowship of the Ring' and the first half of 'The Two Towers.' The final movie was called 'The Return of the King', and covered the second half of 'The Two Towers' and 'The Return of the King' entirely. Why would anyone establish such an absurd breakdown of the storyline? Any Tolkien fan knew that the story consisted of four books. He and Melissa had discussed this many times. Vinny pushed this last thought from his mind and was relieved to feel his eyes were completely dry.

He replaced one tape after the other automatically, and, before realizing it, had gone through all three movies. It was nearly ten o'clock when he had finished rewinding the last tape. He had spent the entire time analyzing the differences between the novel and film versions, and he suddenly realized that he had not thought about Melissa in several hours. Maybe this birthday would not turn out to be such a disaster after all.

Vinny had been born at 11.55 p.m., and it had always been a tradition in his family to celebrate at the exact hour, and not a minute before. If he got ready now, he could be in the Village by 11.30 p.m. and find a spot to celebrate. But where would he go? His friends had suggested a hot new club called Fantasy but, as usual, he had turned them down, and said it was not for him. He thought about calling his friends, and then changed his mind. He had made the decision to start a new life today, but was not in the mood to go into lengthy explanations of what his reasons were, and he knew that his friends would never leave it alone. He dressed quickly and glanced at himself in the mirror.

"It's going to be OK, Vinny," he said to his reflection and left the apartment.

During his subway ride into the city, he was in good spirits, and even looking forward to his night out, but as soon as he was half a block away from the club, he began having second thoughts. *I am no good in social situations*, he thought nervously. Then again, from what his friends had told him, the aptly named Fantasy was not known for its deep socialization practices. Basically, a man would have a raging erection by the time he had his second drink and look for the nearest woman not wearing any underwear that was willing to follow him into a dark corner for a cheap thrill, no strings attached. The man-woman example was not to say that same-gender hook-ups did not take place as well. Fantasy certainly did not discriminate, but the regular crowd was generally straight, young, and extremely horny. This was all good and well as a fantasy, but, somehow for Vinny, the real thing did not seem quite as attractive.

Vinny dragged his feet along the pavement. The club was just around the corner, and another dreadful thought entered his mind. What if this was one of those places where they looked you up and down at the entrance and depending on how cool you looked, they either let you in or sent you away? Vinny may have been an attractive young man, but he was not the world's sharpest dresser, and he certainly did not exude an essence of cool. It would be so humiliating to wait on line for an hour, only to be turned away.

Vinny turned the corner, and, as if in response to his thoughts, saw a long line and three young men arguing with the bouncer at the head. The bouncer was an enormous black man who stood about six-foot-eight, and had to weigh at least two hundred seventy-five pounds, maybe even three hundred. The tallest of the young men might have been six feet tall if you were feeling particularly generous, but he was raising his voice to the bouncer with a lot of confidence.

"I don't give a shit *who* your father is. You're not getting in," the bouncer said calmly. His meticulously-shaved head and goatee made him look even more menacing.

Vinny did not think these young men looked uncool at all, quite the contrary. Obviously, the monster guarding the entrance disagreed. Vinny looked at his own garments and slowed down his pace even more.

The young man doing the most vehement arguing was close to the point of exasperation. He had apparently been on the line for forty-five minutes and was not willing to take no for an answer.

"We'll see what the club owner thinks about your attitude. I'm calling my father. Fucking nigger."

These last two words were mumbled under his breath, but loud enough for Vinny to hear. Apparently, the young man's companions also heard because they instinctively took a couple of steps away from their friend. The bouncer took a deep, audible breath. Anticipating trouble, Vinny walked quickly past them in the direction of the back of the line, but the temptation to know what would happen was too great, and he looked around.

As the young man reached into his blazer for his cell phone, the bouncer brought his own head down suddenly. There was a gruesome crunching sound as the bouncer's head connected with the young man's nose, breaking it. The young man staggered backwards and fell off the curb of the sidewalk clutching his nose and howling in pain.

"You broke my fucking nose!" he screamed.

The bouncer walked toward him with the patience of Michael Myers going after Laurie Strode in the Halloween movies. The young man said something else, but Vinny could not understand it through the blood and tears that had almost completely covered his face. The bouncer then grabbed the young man by the hair, lifted him up to face level, and then kneed him savagely in the stomach. The young man went sprawling again and landed on his back. Vinny heard another loud crunch but did not want to guess what had been broken this time.

The initial silence of the crowd when the argument had started was totally gone. A cacophony of murmurs, gasps, screams, and even laughter dominated the air around Vinny. He was horrified by what he was seeing, but unable to look away. A strange sort of hypnosis had come over him. A woman in the crowd yelled hysterically, "Someone help! He's killing him!"

Other bouncers had now come out into the street, trying in vain to hold back the gargantuan black man. By this time, the unfortunate young man who had carelessly let out the racial slur was not much more than a bloody pulp, grotesquely reminding Vinny of the classic, science-fiction movie, 'The Blob.'

In their attempt to control the angry bouncer, his colleagues had left the entrance to the club unguarded, and people started to leave the line, and take advantage of the opportunity. The sudden massive movement away from the fight seemed to wake Vinny up from his trance. Finally tearing his gaze away from the violent scene, Vinny followed their lead and entered the club with no resistance whatsoever.

Once inside, it was amazingly easy to forget the event that had so captured his attention only a few moments ago. The club was packed. The music was blaring, and the dancing was so sexual in nature that Vinny felt overwhelmed. No amount of foreplay he had experienced, or even seen on films, could measure up to what he was witnessing at this moment. The couples on the dance floor were as free and uninhibited with their hands and mouths on each other as if they were in the privacy of their own bedrooms. Vinny gawked at them for what seemed like hours, but they paid him no mind. Occasionally they would step on him or bump into him, but he may as well have just been a wall column in the room.

Suddenly, he saw something that caught his attention. At the far end of the crescent-shaped bar he noticed a man studying the crowd with almost scientific interest. His style was unique. He was all dressed in black. He had leather, steel-toed boots, leather pants and a silk shirt. He had long, black hair that went down to his waist in a French braid, piercing black eyes and black, stud earrings in both ears. The way he was sitting denoted class, but also a sort of mysterious edge that simultaneously made him look rugged. *I bet he had no problem passing the bouncer's coolness test*, thought Vinny. Next to him there was an empty barstool. Vinny hesitated a bit and walked toward it. He sat down next to the mysterious man who showed absolutely no sign of noticing his presence and addressed the bartender.

"Excuse me, miss?"

She was a voluptuous blonde with skintight jeans and a halter-top that barely covered her massive breasts.

"What can I get you, handsome?"

For some inexplicable reason, this suddenly seemed to be an extremely complex question. Vinny was not really a drinker. He had never acquired a taste for hard liquor but thought it inappropriate to ask for a glass of wine in such a place. While this thought process was going on in Vinny's head, the bartender eyed him with the hunger of a ravenous beast. She stretched her arms above her head, and then leaned up against the bar to ensure he got an eyeful of her feminine charms. Of course, Vinny was too lost in thought trying to figure out what seemed to be the most difficult decision of his life. He wanted to appear savvy, and not overwhelmed by his current surroundings. He would stick to beer. Beer was always the safest bet. He would choose an imported beer, just to appear a bit more sophisticated.

"Heineken."

Vinny was suddenly confused. Had he said that out loud, or was his inner voice that deep and secure?

"Coming right up, sexy," the bartender beamed.

She turned around ceremoniously and made sure to bend down long enough, so that there would be no doubt with respect to the color of the thong she was wearing. She then popped the top open on the bottle and handed the darkly clad stranger next to Vinny an ice-cold Heineken. The man hardly moved at all. He simply took the bottle, and gave her a quick, casual wink. Vinny thought it was the coolest gesture he had ever seen, either in real life or on screen, and was in awe despite himself. The man was in total control of the moment. Apparently, the voluptuous blonde felt very much the same because she looked about ready to explode with ecstasy; her momentary interest in Vinny now totally forgotten.

Vinny turned to the stranger.

"It looks like you just made her night."

The man did not even look at Vinny. He continued to study the crowd.

"She won't feel the same when I leave, and there is no tip."

With that he just took a couple of sips of his beer, laid out six one-dollar bills on the bar, and left without another word. Vinny looked above the bar and saw that the price of imported beer was exactly six dollars a bottle. The man had not been kidding about not leaving a tip, but Vinny was sure that the bartender would not even notice the fact. Vinny suddenly felt a strange urge to go after him. He did not know why, but he felt it was important for him that he got to know this character. He started walking after him and was about to call him.

"Hey, wait!" the bartender yelled out.

Both Vinny and the man in black turned around at the same time. She had come around the bar and was now standing in the middle of the crowd in all her sexy splendor. She flashed a gorgeous smile and opened her eyes wide.

"When will I see you again?"

For a brief, ridiculous moment Vinny thought she was talking to him, and stupidly raised his hand to his chest as if to ask, *Who? Me?* He quickly realized she was looking past him and lowered his hand in what only *he* thought was a casual manner. He could feel the scorching heat of embarrassment rise to his face.

"One of these days," the mysterious man in the French braid answered.

He blew her a kiss, and she was transformed from club vixen to giggly schoolgirl in a matter of seconds. He then turned around and was on his way again, leaving the bartender as well as several club goers, both male and female, to stare longingly at him.

Vinny followed him all the way out of the club and into the street. He did not know how to approach him, so he said the first thing to come to mind.

"Excuse me, sir. Do you have the time?"

The man looked at Vinny's wrist.

"Is your watch not working?"

Vinny looked at his wrist uncomfortably.

"I meant a light. Do you have a light?"

"I don't smoke," the man said suspiciously, taking a cautious step back from Vinny. Vinny just looked around, feeling more and more uncomfortable by the second. He stuffed his hands into his pockets.

"Look, man. I'm straight," the man said slowly as if speaking to a child. "There's a club a few blocks up where you can find…"

Vinny suddenly realized the direction this was taking and did not like it one bit.

"I'm not hitting on you," he said defensively.

"Whatever you say, friend," the man said and started to walk away.

This was a fine mess Vinny had gotten himself into. Now he had to defend his sexuality to a stranger. He should never have gone out tonight. It was a stupid idea, and now even stupider things were happening because of it. All he had wanted to do was to start a new life by celebrating his twenty-fifth birthday in a different way. He wanted to scream, laugh and cry, all at the same time.

"It's my birthday," he said stupidly.

That was a stroke of genius if there ever was one. That would explain everything to the man he had just met. After all, gay stalkers and birthday boys were always being mistaken for one another on the streets of New York. The stranger turned around and a cynical, almost evil smile curled up on his lips as Vinny grappled with his thoughts. The initial apprehension was gone from his eyes and he simply said, "Well, why didn't you say so? Let's go celebrate."

Vinny just stared at him, uncomprehending. The man put a fraternal arm around him and started leading him away from the club. Vinny looked back at Fantasy and the dark-haired stranger told him to forget about them, because they were a sorry bunch of repressed losers. Vinny allowed himself to be guided away by his new friend. He led him down a few dark streets and turned several corners with the ease of an infantry soldier wearing night-vision goggles. They finally came to what appeared to be a dead-end street. Now it was Vinny's turn to be nervous, and it could be read clearly on his face.

"Relax, birthday boy," the man said. "By the way, I'm Vic."

He stuck out his hand. Shaking his hand suddenly made Vinny feel at ease. This was no longer a stranger. This was his new friend, Vic, who could melt the hottest of girls with the wink of an eye and a few careless words. If there was anyone he wanted by his side for the new beginning of his new life, it was Vic.

"Vinny," he said and smiled.

"All right, Vinny," Vic said warmly, "what time were you born?"

Vinny looked at his wrist. The watch read 11.55 p.m., and he showed it to Vic.

"At this exact hour, as a matter of fact."

"Let's get this party started, then. Happy birthday, man."

They walked together to the high brick wall at the end of the street, and Vinny noticed that there was a bomb shelter entrance off to the left. The doors had been painted the same color as the street, so it was not obvious unless you were looking for it. Vic went to the doors and tugged them upward and open ceremoniously.

"After you, sir," he said, making a graceful gesture with his arms.

Vinny walked down the concrete steps, and Vic followed suit, closing the doors behind them. Underground, there was a long, narrow tunnel dimly lit with a few ancient-looking bulbs placed along both sides of the wall. It ended in a small staircase that had a gigantic, metallic door painted bright red. Vic walked up the steps and knocked on the door in a succession that might have been Morse code. The door creaked open, and Vinny immediately heard the lulling, sensual sound of the music of Enigma pulsing out. A tall, well-built man with long blond hair nodded courteously at Vic and moved aside to allow Vic and Vinny access to the underground club.

Vinny had been stunned by the ambience at Fantasy, but he obviously had a lot to learn. This club seemed to be a combination of new age and gothic, rolled into one. Everybody here, both men and women, were gorgeous. Vic walked up to one of the cage dancers, and whispered in her ear. She giggled sensually and followed him down to where Vinny was standing.

"Valentina would like to give the birthday boy a kiss," he said slyly.

She walked over to Vinny and he opened his arms in a friendly embrace. Valentina was a petite Latina with a body full of curves, full red lips, and fire in her eyes. She ignored the arms completely, and jumped up onto Vinny, hooking her arms around his neck and wrapping her legs around his back. She then kissed him voraciously as she pressed herself against him and moaned sensually. Vinny's body was on fire, and as it began to show, he made no effort to conceal it. This seemed to excite Valentina even more. She jumped off him and quick as lightning, she was down on her knees, unzipping his pants. Vinny knew what was going to happen now. He wanted desperately for it *to* happen, but when it was taking place, he could not believe that it *was* happening. He looked down and saw only the top of Valentina's head, moving back and forth in a steady, pulsing motion. Vinny looked over at Vic who simply grinned. He then left Vinny to enjoy the rest of his special birthday present. It seemed to Vinny that he was standing there forever. At one point, a red-haired

31

waitress in sexy lingerie asked him if he wanted a drink, completely ignoring the act going on right beside her. Vinny declined politely as he felt that Valentina was still going strong. When they were done, Valentina zipped up his pants, and said almost shyly, "I have to get back to work. Happy birthday, Vinny."

With this she went back to her cage, and continued dancing as if she had just come back from a cigarette break.

Vinny walked around the club in awe. Everywhere he looked there was at least a couple or a group of people having sex, and this was not what his friends liked to call *dry humping* when they went to clubs. This was full-on, free-style, no-holds-barred *fucking*. The people at Fantasy seemed shy by comparison. After walking around for a few minutes, he finally spotted Vic. He was with a group of young girls that seemed to have come straight out of a movie about horny college co-eds and their wild dorm room escapades. On a low table there was a bare-chested girl lying on her back. Vic would pour shots of tequila on her from mouth to navel, and his two other female companions would then take turns, girls making out with the girl on the table and licking the liquor off her body. Vic did not seem to be particularly enjoying the game, and Vinny wondered why he was not taking a more active part in it.

"Why don't you join in?"

Vic looked up with a weary smile.

"I have to save my energy for later, but if you feel so inclined, by all means," he said pointing to the threesome as if showing off a prized sculpture.

"Thank you, but I think your friend Valentina sucked the energy right out of me."

They both burst out laughing at Vinny's unintentional, but

ever-so-appropriate, choice of words.

"Let's get out of here," Vic said. "I want you to see my place upstairs."

"You live here?"

"Don't we all at some point or another?"

Vinny had no idea what that meant but decided to follow Vic anyway when he got up. "Good night, ladies."

"Bye, Vic!" the girls answered in a giggly, drunken chorus.

"It's Vinny!" he yelled at them ferociously, but they were too far gone to even notice. This was the first time Vinny had seen Vic lose his composure.

"I think they were talking to you, Vic."

Vic seemed to relax a little at this although he still appeared upset.

"These sluts are too fucking shallow and stupid to even know who they're talking to. Come on. Let's go."

Vinny followed Vic up a winding staircase. Vic opened the door and said to Vinny, "After you. Tu casa es mi casa."

Vinny had not studied Spanish since high school, but he clearly remembered the saying being *Mi casa es tu casa.* Vic had switched the possessives. Why had he done that? Perhaps he did not know.

But when Vinny heard the door slam violently behind him and saw Vic standing in front of it protectively, he realized there had been no error in the use of the language. Vinny was standing in the middle of his own studio apartment and Vic was staring coldly at him.

"What is this?" he asked perplexed. "How did we get here?"

"There's no time now. We need to do this quickly."

Vic walked over to Vinny and grabbed him by the elbow. Vinny shook him off violently. "Time for what? Do what quickly? What the fuck is going on?"

Vic continued looking at him with a cold stare, but now there seemed to be a hint of impatience, and even hatred in his eyes as well. Vinny's head was spinning.

"I mean, one minute I'm having the best night of my pathetic life, and then I'm suddenly back in my embarrassingly tiny studio."

Vic's fist came out fast as lightning and hit Vinny square on the jaw so hard that it knocked him down. Vinny stared up at Vic in a daze of pain and confusion. Vic squatted down to where Vinny was, and looked at him with more glowering hatred than before.

"Listen to me carefully, you ungrateful piece of shit. You have no idea how lucky you are. You're always so busy bitching about your existence that you don't ever take your head out of your ass long enough to look around you. This was not my vision. I allowed you to get away from me, but all that ends now."

What vision? What ends now? What is this psycho talking about? Vinny's thoughts were a whirlwind of confusion. *How could this man possibly be jealous of me?* Vinny wondered. He had heard about the grass always being greener on the other side, but that could certainly not apply to the two of them. Vic had it all. Looks. Style. Grace. Confidence.

As if reading Vinny's thoughts, Vic took a deep breath, trying to control his anger.

"You have a great little apartment, a steady paycheck and a dear, sweet, old mother back home that loves you."

He seemed to consider something for a moment and then added, "You even had a beautiful girlfriend, but you blew it."

This last part made Vinny extremely angry.

"What girlfriend?" he spat at Vic. "That little whore…"

Vic did not allow him to finish. He grabbed Vinny's injured jaw with his right hand and forced his mouth shut by pushing his chin up. Tears of pain and fear rolled down Vinny's cheeks.

"Melissa…" Vic said slowly, "was simply not ready for your overeager bullshit. But don't worry. I am going to fix everything."

He then released his jaw and grasped both of Vinny's temples with his hands, pressing against them extremely hard. Vinny put his own hands on Vic's shoulders, trying to push him away, but Vic was too strong. The apartment started trembling all around them, and Vinny's vision began to blur. He thought he heard voices around him but was not sure where they were coming from. Vinny began to scream.

"Shut up! I need to concentrate!" Vic roared at Vinny. "It won't work if I don't concentrate. Shut the fuck up!"

Vinny continued screaming hysterically, and soon, Vic and Vinny's screams merged into a single, almost inhuman howl.

"Clear!" the male voice said, and Vic felt a sharp, hot pain in his chest.

"Clear!" the same voice repeated in a sharper tone.

Vic felt the pain again and groggily opened his eyes. There were potent florescent lights above him and people in surgical masks all around him. In the distance, he could hear a faint beeping sound change from fast, consecutive tones to a slow steady rhythm.

"He's back, doctor!" a female voice exclaimed.

There was an audible, collective sigh of relief in the operating room.

"No!" Vic whispered weakly. "I just needed a few more seconds. Just a few more seconds."

Large tears streamed down his face.

"Oh my God, doctor. He's awake!" the same female voice said with concern.

"Just give him another shot of anesthesia. It happens sometimes toward the end of a complex procedure like this one," the male voice answered calmly.

Vic immediately began feeling drowsier than he already was. *I was so close. I was so damn close*, he thought as the world faded to black.

A beautiful young nurse walked into the doctor's office. She locked the door behind her and took off her cap, allowing her gorgeous brown hair to fall over her shoulders. She then walked over to the handsome young doctor sitting on the edge of the desk. They hugged and kissed passionately.

"Congratulations, Dr. Falcon. Another successful surgery," she said coquettishly.

"I couldn't have done it without you, Nurse Sandino," he answered, and they kissed again.

"You know," Sandino said, ruffling Falcon's hair, "you may have saved the world's next Nobel Prize for Literature. I think he is a writer."

"Now, how could you possibly know that?"

"Because he had a notebook on him when they brought him in. I think he's writing some sort of autobiography. It's about a shy young man from New Jersey named Vincent who comes to New York in search of a new life."

"Well, first off, that's not our guy. Our twenty-five-year-old male's name is Victor and he's a local. He took two bullets in the chest when an exotic dancer's boyfriend caught her waxing his pole in a club downtown. Doesn't sound too shy to me."

Sandino looked at Falcon in genuine surprise.

"Well, I guess it's not an autobiography after all. It just felt so personal, you know?"

"And secondly, speaking of personal, you're a very naughty little nurse, going through a patient's personal effects like that."

"You're right," she answered, lowering her gaze momentarily in mock shame. "But you like me naughty, don't you doctor?" She offered him an inviting smile.

Falcon returned the smile. "So where are we going tonight, babe?" he asked, putting his arms around her waist.

"I hear Fantasy is the hottest new club downtown. Why don't we go check it out?" Sandino suggested.

"Sounds good to me," Falcon agreed, and they walked out of the office with their arms around each other's waists.

First Impressions

Throughout our lives, we are many times told that we should not judge a book by its cover, and that first impressions are not necessarily trustworthy. However, what we are rarely told is that on many occasions, a book's cover may offer a perfectly accurate representation of its contents, and that for some of us, first impressions should be taken very seriously because they will, more often than not, end up being correct.

This was the case when I first saw her. The university where I taught was holding its annual, end-of-term social event. Academic departments rotated the organization of the event every semester, so it would usually end up becoming a fierce competition to see which department could outdo the others in solidifying the university's image as a welcoming environment for faculty, staff, and students alike.

My department, and our chairperson in particular, were pulling out all the stops this year. We were courting a local nonagenarian who was not only an alumnus but had more money than he knew what to do with. He had recently expressed interest in donating a large sum of money to the university, but he wanted the academic departments to compete for it and compete we did. It was like a battle royale where, although alliances were temporarily formed with a common goal in mind, they were just as easily dissolved, as only one department would be left standing at the end to claim the grand prize.

Our fearless leader in this blood sport was Professor

Grossman, chair of the Department of Media Studies. During our last faculty meeting, he had made it clear that he expected all of us to not only attend the event, but to be active participants throughout the night.

"Listen up, guys. Old man Brown is going the way of Shakespeare's expiring frog, so we have to act now," he explained with all the finesse and charm of a used car salesman.

Professor Gerard expelled a sound which was an eerie combination of cough, snort and chuckle accompanied by a face of total disgust and indignation.

"I believe you meant to reference Dickens, not Shakespeare."

Gerard was a frustrated literature professor who had been turned down three times by the English Department at Riverdale University until he finally settled for teaching communication theory courses.

Grossman was not in the least put out by the interruption.

"Whatever. My point is we need to kiss this guy's ass before he becomes a corpse if we want the money for the new television studio. We must be the only campus in New York that is still shooting in SD. Everybody else has gone HD. It's embarrassing."

This last comment met with a generalized murmur of agreement from the group.

"And when I say kiss his ass…" he continued, emboldened by the show of support, "I don't mean a chaste, first-date kiss between five-year-olds. I mean a deep-tongue, saliva-swapping, hormone-filled, teen-angst, French kiss that will haunt his erotic dreams until he finally drops dead."

Unlike his previous comment, this one was met with mixed reviews. A few hearty laughs were heard. Most just let out a perfunctory giggle but seemed more embarrassed than shocked.

I was more than a bit disturbed that he thought first dates took place at age five, but perhaps he was talking from personal experience, and, knowing Grossman, that would not surprise me at all.

He went on to explain that it would not be enough to simply attend the event. As we were the organizing department, we would all be given specific tasks to perform during the evening. Although we had more than enough budget to cover professional catering services, Grossman thought that having faculty and staff as servers would add a personal touch and show some humility, hopefully clinching the deal for Brown's money.

The suggestion met with some resistance, but we finally all agreed that it was for the greater good and were assigned individual tasks. I was designated bartender for the event. I suppose the fact that I had completed four out of the twelve hours needed for bartending school eight years ago made me the most qualified of the group. My only competition was Professor Dante, who taught photography, was a known alcoholic, and claimed to do his best work when drunk. I was awarded the coveted position. My training consisted of a quick perusal of Bartending for Dummies and my limited knowledge of mixology. Thus, I prepared myself for being thrown into the fire for my bartending debut on campus.

The event was scheduled for a Thursday evening in late May and the weather was already beginning to show signs of summer. As the Department of Media Studies was hosting this time around, the set-up was impressive. We set up our aging television studio in such a way that provided an aesthetic proscenium for the event as well as clearly showcasing the dire need for a technology upgrade. Floor cameras that had been the latest trend when Kennedy was president, playback decks for vinyl, 8-tracks and audiocassettes, and 16mm film splicing machines that any self-respecting editor would now only use as a paper cutter served as props for the chosen theme which was 'Timeless Art.' We received many compliments from faculty outside our department who found our decoration to be very retro chic. If they had known that some of the equipment was still being used for production classes, they would not have been as impressed.

Resigned to my fate as a non-professional bartender for the night, I was looking over my mixology cheat sheet and sweating profusely under the overhead studio lights that had been arranged by Professor Gianni, our resident lighting director, to hover over the bar area. I heard him say to me, "Hot enough for you, Victor?"

As these words left his mouth, he licked his lips and eyed me as someone who is salivating over a juicy piece of steak. In a space of a few seconds, I thought of several comebacks that would finally convince this man that I was not interested. He had been asking me out all semester, and I had politely declined every single time, reminding him that I was straight, but he kept on insisting and pointing out the fact that he had once been straight as well. Just when I was about to answer something, no doubt clever, that I can no longer recall, I saw her for the first time.

Gianni saw that my attention was otherwise engaged and left in a huff, mumbling something about men being more trouble than they were worth under his breath. Although admittedly a lapse in basic manners, I completely ignored him, and focused on the beauty approaching the bar. She was of medium height with white, satiny skin and long, straight blonde hair that went down to her waist. The skin-tight jeans she wore hugged every voluptuous curve of her lower body and the cut-off t-shirt she had on exposed a perfectly flat abdomen that led up to an ample bosom. As she walked, the big, hoop earrings and multiple bracelets she wore jingled and sparkled to the tune of an imaginary rhythm that no doubt accompanied her movements. When she reached the bar, I saw that she had beautiful green eyes that gave her face a feline quality, and complemented her pearly white teeth when she offered me the first of many dazzling smiles to come that would quicken my pulse, ignite my passion, and cloud my judgment.

The first words to come out of her mouth were a perfectly normal greeting followed by, "Sex on the Beach?"

Although I am certainly not trying to make excuses for myself, it is important to understand my general state at that precise moment in time. I was drenched in sweat, mildly annoyed about being hit on by Gianni for the umpteenth time, and absolutely hypnotized by the alluring woman standing before me. The words came tumbling out of my mouth like a waterfall. To this day, I wonder what could have possibly possessed me to respond in such a way that was completely out of character for me.

"OK. If there is no traffic, we can make it to Orchard Beach in less than thirty minutes."

I can honestly say that it was the first time I had been so bold, for lack of a better word, in my dealings with women. There are some men who have a natural ability when it comes to engaging a woman's interest. It is a complex dance that I never learned the steps to, and the fact that I was a bit of a recluse certainly did not help. All of this is not to say that I had not enjoyed the company of women throughout my life. I had had more than my fair share of romantic encounters, the common factors among them being the generally short lifespan of the relationships, and the fact that the times that I made the first move were few and far between.

This can probably be traced back to the fact that I had a relatively uneventful upbringing. I grew up in the Riverdale area of New York. Those that are familiar with New York geography know that Riverdale is undeniably and unequivocally located in the Bronx. However, people from the area will always say they live in Riverdale, much in the same way that people from Manhattan will obnoxiously proclaim that they live in the city, as if the other boroughs did not deserve this distinction. Geopolitics aside, both my parents came from wealthy families that had immigrated to New York in the first half of the twentieth century and set themselves up comfortably in the area. Although I never doubted that my parents cared for me, I cannot say that there were any particularly strong emotional ties between us. All my needs were provided for, and I led a comfortable life at home. My parents traveled quite a bit for work and after retirement, continued doing so for pleasure. I never even considered moving out as I would have the run of the entire house on a regular basis, sometimes even for months on end.

Although I never overtly blamed my parents for my shyness, I do think that our lack of communication contributed significantly to my introverted personality. I spent so much time alone as a child that I got quite comfortable with my solitude. Boredom was rarely an issue. I was a very artistic person and would find a plethora of different creative activities to pass the time. My passion for the fine arts grew from my need to express myself and the visual arts provided a perfect outlet to do so. By the time I reached high school, I had successfully developed a tortured artist persona, which suited me perfectly as people generally left me alone. My comfortable existence at home, and my general live and let live attitude toward others, provided few opportunities for genuine artistic suffering, but it was a convenient façade which I wore well and used to my advantage.

Far from projecting the image of a dark, brooding artist the night I first met her, I instead came across as a blithering idiot with my poor choice of words. My first impulse was to apologize, but I never got the chance. She looked at me with a strange combination of incredulity and amusement, although she did not seem particularly offended. However, her only words to me were a drawn out, "OK, then," and she walked away in all her exotic splendor.

"Jackass!" I admonished myself severely. "What on earth were you thinking?"

Luckily, the rest of the night was not nearly as disastrous and turned out to be quite enjoyable. Grossman acted as MC and made the attendees blush with his off-color jokes, but once the alcohol started flowing, the crowd warmed up to his style. Even though it was not intended to be an actual party, there were some people dancing, and toward the end of the evening, there were enough pairings going on to provide fodder for those interested in water-cooler gossip. I saw her several times more throughout the night and tried to read any sort of reaction to my unfortunate comment on her face but was unsuccessful.

She appeared to be sociable enough with everyone, albeit in a politely distant manner. She declined several offers to dance with an apologetic smile, and her presence at the event was noticed by men and women alike. She really was an insanely attractive woman, and I was mesmerized, but there were two words that kept forcing themselves into my brain, as much as I tried to keep them out. The first one was *ghetto*. I realized it was a snap judgment, and I even felt guilty for thinking it, but I could not help it. There it was in my head, like a glowing neon sign in Las Vegas. The one that immediately followed it was *danger*. In hindsight, I feel that ignoring the former was probably unwise, although I could easily justify it with arguments of social equality and the power of love. However, not paying heed to the latter was a mistake that I would live to regret for the rest of my life.

After that evening, everything seemed to fall into place for the Media Studies Department. We received a large, monetary donation from Brown who appreciated our salt of the earth approach to entertaining. Apparently, Grossman had hit a home run with this one. The money would be used for a total upgrade of the television studio, with enough left over to replace all our archaic field equipment with brand-spanking, shiny, new gadgets. As a full-time faculty member, it was expected of me to be around during the summer, or at least on call if I was needed. However, since most of my work took place in the studio, and the renovation process would be quite hectic, I was given a whole three months off at full pay. The audiovisual engineers insisted on overseeing the project themselves, so I would not have to back on campus until after Labor Day.

It could not get much better than this, except that it did. I spoke to my parents about my windfall, and they suggested that I do some traveling during the summer. I was up for tenure review in the fall, and it would be a good way for me to relax and prepare myself, both physically and psychologically. I was not to worry about anything because all my expenses would be covered. Touched by their generosity, I was tempted to tell them that a week on an island would be more than sufficient, but instead we agreed that a ninety-day tour of Latin America was in order. Although I had traveled extensively throughout Europe and the Caribbean, I had never explored the American continent south of Mexico, and my parents thought that this would be the perfect opportunity to do so. Being the dutiful son that I was, I accepted.

To say that I enjoyed myself that summer would be a wild understatement. Timid as I was, I found it quite easy to make friends during this time. Of course, I did not really need to make much of an effort. I was constantly approached by people wherever I went. My muscular physique, long, black hair and blue eyes caused quite the sensation with the locals. I was an especially big hit with the ladies. Once they found out that I was an American citizen, my attractiveness seemed to soar to dizzying heights.

Many would meet me, and, in the space of a few hours, have sex with me, declare their undying love and propose marriage, not necessarily in that order. The common narratives were that they *were not that type of girl, did not understand what had happened to them with me* and *had never done anything like this before with anyone else.* Throughout the summer, I would sometimes meet fellow travelers, generally from the United Kingdom, Australia, New Zealand, Canada, and the United States with similar stories. On several occasions, they even involved the same women, so it became a kind of running joke among us.

Did I take full advantage of the situation? Absolutely. Did I feel guilty about it? Not in the least. I never once lied to any of the women that I met. They all knew that I was on vacation, and I certainly never promised to take any of them back with me to the United States. We were consenting adults and that was that. In the three months that I traveled throughout Latin America, I had more romantic encounters than I had had in my almost thirty years on the planet up to date. My thought process was that I might as well enjoy myself while there were no real consequences for my actions. Once I returned to New York, I would have to deal with the same group of people on a regular basis, especially if I got tenure.

I returned to Riverdale University, rested but pleasantly exhausted at the same time, with a clear mind and the firm intention of focusing on my upcoming tenure review. Achieving lifetime employment at a university had never been in my plans. Although I knew myself to be a good professor, I would never claim to be a great one. My expectations were straightforward and students either fulfilled the requirements or they did not and were graded accordingly. I did not believe in any type of outreach or integration with students. I was polite enough not to be considered arrogant but made no effort to become their friend. If they requested advice or help, I would give it, but never actually offered it, and as far as I was concerned, my obligation to students ended once they were no longer taking my classes.

The Media Studies Department did not really care for my attitude but tolerated it because all the creative work I had done, since being affiliated to the college, had the Riverdale University name attached to it. Since my early days as an undergraduate student at the college, my work had received several local, national, and even international awards that translated into funding for the department and overall prestige for the university.

Some of my colleagues did not much appreciate my position in the department either. I had gone straight through my education at Riverdale University: Bachelor of Arts at twenty-two, Master of Fine Arts at twenty-four, faculty appointment three days after my graduation ceremony, and at twenty-nine I was already eligible for my first tenure review. If successful, I would be the only professor under thirty to get tenure in the Department of Media Studies. On top of that, more than a few of them had been my professors, both in the undergraduate and graduate programs, and less than a decade later, we were colleagues.

I was marginally proud of my academic achievements because I felt I was making an intelligent career choice as far as stability was concerned. Although I was good at it, I was certainly not passionate about teaching. However, my position at the university allowed me the freedom to pursue my artistic endeavors, which I *was* passionate about, with full funding. Sometimes I was considered a sellout for not breaking away from the safety of the university, and going off on my own, but, truth be told, I was a naturally lazy person, so my situation suited me perfectly.

During my summer of sexual debauchery, I would be lying if I said that the image of the girl at the end-of-semester event did not enter my mind on more than one occasion. The initial embarrassment I had felt upon our first encounter was now a distant memory, but she had undoubtedly made an impression on me, so much so that when I saw her again, I was once again caught completely off guard.

One of the residual consequences of my Latin American trip was that I had lost my voice the weekend before classes started up again. For someone like me, who was unaccustomed to heavy partying in clubs, the regular consumption of alcohol, together with having to scream over loud music to be heard did quite a number on my throat. The doctor gave me some medicine and told me that I would be fine in a few days, but I thought that a voiceless professor would not make a good impression on the first day, so I decided to cancel my first session. I dutifully wrote an explanatory e-mail to my future students, copied the department Academic Coordinator and was all set. I was not particularly concerned. Most students skipped the first week of classes anyway. In fact, all professors were strongly encouraged not to count absences until week three of the semester.

As expected, there were no issues regarding my absence, but I did receive an unexpected e-mail from a student. It read:

Dear Professor Steiner, I am sorry to hear that you are not feeling well. I wish you a speedy recovery and look forward to taking your class. Sincerely, Lina Velasquez.

That was something you did not see every day. At the very least, it merited a cordial response. Without giving it much thought, I responded:

Lina, Thank you for the kind words. Victor Steiner.

I had never been a fan of using terms of endearment to greet strangers or closings that denoted any sort of emotion. It was a basic response form that I always used and had worked well so far.

That semester I was only scheduled to teach one class on Monday evenings. It was determined that the rest of my time be dedicated to research, creative work, and the preparation for my tenure review. In other words, I basically had a free pass for the next four months. The word around campus was that my student evaluations were sound, if not exemplary, but that my portfolio of creative work, done in the university's name, was more than enough to secure my tenure. Making me wait until December was simply a formality, and as long as I showed up to the review it was a done deal.

With the promise of securing an academic position forever before my thirtieth birthday, my spirits were high when the following Monday came along. I walked into the classroom with a bit of a swagger but stopped dead in my tracks when I saw her again. This time she had her hair in a tight ponytail and was wearing a form-fitting, dark blue business suit. The skirt was short enough to show off her beautifully toned legs without being vulgar, and the jacket was tailored in such a way that denoted classiness and sexiness at the same time. Although she answered when I greeted the class, she did not seem to recognize me. *Thank God for small favors*, I thought to myself when I recovered from my initial shock.

First meetings with students are always a low-stress affair. You spend time introducing yourself, having them introduce themselves, and going over very general information that is forgotten within a few hours and rarely used again during the semester. It is a space for light dialogue and light humor that does not really amount to anything. However, for some reason, seeing her again made me nervous, and put me in such a flustered state that I became tongue-tied more than once and had trouble focusing on what I was saying.

Due to my youth and looks, I was used to seeing a few dreamy-eyed students giggling coquettishly from time to time during my classes, especially on the first day, but she looked at me with an intensity that made me very self-conscious. She seemed to hang on my every word but was not being openly flirtatious like some of the others. Even with all the attention I was getting from her, I searched for the slightest trace of recognition in her eyes but found none. *She really does not remember me*, I thought, a little deflated. Of course, when you thought about it, there was no real reason why she should. After all, women that look like that must be hit on a dozen times a day. After a while, the number of clowns that make inappropriate comments must become one giant blur.

When it came time for her to introduce herself, I found out that she was the author of the thoughtful e-mail I had received. I also found out that she had won a full scholarship to Riverdale University for being the student with the highest GPA in the graduating class of her South Bronx high school, and that her dream was to be a television newscaster for a major network in New York. As soon as I heard her speak, I was once again bombarded by the unwelcome terms that had forced themselves into my brain upon our first meeting. This girl was clearly from *the hood*. She was well dressed, although a bit on the sexy side, but her cadence was what my friend Sal would label as *classy ghetto*. In other words, she was keenly aware of her background, but doing her best to move forward.

This, in and of itself, was quite admirable in my opinion. Several acquaintances of mine brushed off my ideas as elitist and retrograde. I was a firm believer that although being *from* the ghetto was nothing to be ashamed of, *being* ghetto was nothing to be proud of either. This girl understood the distinction well, and that made me even more attracted to her than I already was. I wanted to say something encouraging to her to show my support, but I was afraid it might draw more attention to what she was perhaps trying to conceal, so instead I opted for saying, "You're the one who wrote me that kind e-mail. Thank you. I appreciate the gesture."

In response, she smiled demurely and cast down her eyes, as if ashamed of the attention.

The evening continued in the same light manner, but now and again, I would steal a quick glance at Lina and always receive a smile in return. When the session ended, a few students came up to my desk for specific questions, and while answering I kept on eye out for Lina. I did not want her to leave without my noticing it. Not that I planned to do anything about it. As I have explained before, I rarely did, but I was hoping for one last look, and perhaps one of her beautiful smiles before leaving campus. Unfortunately, at some point I must have missed her exiting the classroom because she was nowhere to be found. Disappointed, I said goodnight to the last couple of students after answering their questions and started packing up my things. A couple of minutes later, I saw Lina standing in the doorway in all her sexy splendor.

"Good night, Professor Steiner. I hope you feel better. I wouldn't want to miss out on any of your classes," she said this with a flirty smile which merited a clever response on my part.

"In that case, I will drag myself to class, no matter what ails me from now on."

To this she responded with a laugh and answered, "That's good news. I can tell that you're a great professor."

"Really?" I replied with a slight narrowing of my eyes. "How can you tell from a single session?"

"Call it women's intuition," she answered. "In any event, you are certainly a better professor than you are a bartender."

Another gorgeous smile, casual hair flip, and she was gone.

Exactly how we became a couple is still a mystery to me. There was never a clear transition from one status to the other. Within a matter of weeks, we were already talking about the future in terms of *us*. This was unchartered territory for me. All my life, I had been used to doing whatever I wanted whenever I wanted. This was no longer the case for me. I was responsible for another human being now, or so I would have myself believe. My friend Sal picked up on this immediately, and he was less than impressed with my new outlook on life.

"Pussy-whipped!" he said, poking me forcefully in the chest. "Either that ... or black magic," he continued, considering the alternatives.

"I know it must look that way," I started defending myself.

"It even feels that way sometimes, but I'm telling you, man. This is different. I think that this time, it really is …"

"Swear to God, if your next word is love, I will slap you like the little bitch you've become in the past few weeks. I know she's smoking hot. I realize that the face of an angel on the body of a porn star is a hard combination to resist, but you need to open up your eyes."

"Open them up to what?" I asked, knowing exactly what he meant.

"In the wise words of Tyler Durden, this girl is a predator posing as a house pet. I'm telling you, man. This chic is a walking danger sign."

There was that word again, rearing its ugly head to remind me that *danger* was exactly what I had thought when I first saw her. Of course, I would never admit that to Sal, no matter how strong our friendship was. Instead, I said the first idiotic thing that came into my head.

"You're just jealous."

Admittedly, it was a weak retort, and not based on any evidence of fact, but it did serve to end the conversation. Sal threw up his arms in vexation, gave me a fraternal slap on the cheek, and put his forehead against mine, saying in a soft but firm tone.

"Whatever you say, brother."

He then heaved a deep sigh of disappointment and walked away.

I hated parting on these terms with someone who obviously cared for my well-being. Sal and I had been friends for fifteen years. Our friendship had begun after a fight that left us both bloodied and bruised. I do not recall the actual origin of the argument, but he had called me a Nazi, Kraut bastard to which I had responded in kind, calling him a greasy, Guinea asshole. A shoving match ensued, followed by a flurry of fists and feet. Although I had the height advantage, Sal had the weight advantage, and was quick with his hands. He was able to get in more than a few punches that left me dazed. Finally, after a three-minute altercation that felt like three hours, a school officer broke us up, much to the chagrin of the crowd of spectators that was enjoying the show.

We were both taken to the nurse's office of Riverdale High School, but, as she was busy with a student who had cracked his head trying to perform a skateboard stunt on the railing, we had to wait in the outer office. At this point, we felt it our sacred duty to initially glower at each other, but we had already released our tension during the bout and were no longer angry.

Sal broke the ice first.

"Where did you learn that Van Damme shit you pulled on me in the yard?"

He was referring to a couple of particularly impressive roundhouse kicks that had sent him sprawling to the ground. I explained that I was taking martial arts classes a couple of nights a week and every other Saturday. He seemed interested and followed up with, "You think you can teach me some of those moves?"

I was quite impressed with his punching speed and fancy footwork myself, so I answered, "Only if you show me some of that Tyson magic that left me gasping for breath more than once."

It turns out that Sal's father had been an amateur boxer in the Bronx, so he and his brothers had all reaped the benefit of the paternal experience.

"Deal," answered Sal with the slight trace of a smile as he extended his hand out to me.

I, in return, clasped it firmly with a laugh and from that moment on we were like brothers.

I felt I was somehow betraying Sal by not taking his advice regarding Lina, but I did not want to accept the reality which he was pointing out to me. The fact is that although it had only been a few weeks, I was falling in love with her. I was falling fast, and I was falling hard.

My relationship with Lina was intense, to say the least. I sometimes hesitate to even call it a relationship. It was more of a series of events that took place between two people in an extremely short space of time. Some were positive. Some were negative. All were memorable, albeit for vastly different reasons.

The one that I still, to this day, regardless of all that has happened, hold on to with some nostalgia, is our first kiss. It was early November. Classes had been in session for a couple of months now and everything had settled into a comfortable routine. Lina and I had exchanged some flirty glances, and a couple of cups of coffee, but we had not yet crossed any obvious lines until the previous week.

I had offered to drive her home after class. She had an impractical combination of a subway, bus and walking commute to get home, and this was probably not the safest scenario considering our class let out at almost 10.00 p.m. Many would argue that a true gentleman would not have allowed two months to pass before offering this show of gallantry, but, as I stated before, I was naturally lazy and the South Bronx neighborhood she lived in was out of the way for me. In addition, I felt that if I did it once, I would feel obligated to continue doing it, and on this point at least, I was right.

When we entered her neighborhood, I was welcomed by every possible stereotype I could imagine. Shifty-eyed people standing on street corners, loud music blaring from car stereos, even at this late hour on a weeknight, people having conversations out of their windows or fire escapes, and the enticing smell of Latin American dishes being prepared. We drove up to the front of her building, and, out of habit, I was about to offer to walk her to her door but looked at my surroundings and wondered if it was a good idea. Lina must have noticed my hesitation because she said, "Right here is fine. Thank you so much for the ride."

I half-heartedly started to protest until she added.

"If you walk me in, you won't have a car waiting for you when you come back out."

I did not know if she was joking or not, but I seized the opportunity to say good night. We looked at each other for a moment and then Lina held out her hand. I took it, and she held it for a moment before leaning in and giving me a peck on the cheek. This might have been innocent enough except for the fact that it was extremely close to the corner of my mouth, and that her lips lingered there for a little too long. Although I certainly did not mind on a personal level, I did feel that the limits of propriety had been blurred. However, I quickly told myself that this was not a big deal and, with a smile on my face, bade her good night once again.

I would be lying if I said that on my way home and for several hours afterwards, I did not replay that scene repeatedly in my mind. Sometimes it was in real time. Many times, it included freeze frames and slow motion. In some cases, I even added incidental music or an appropriate soundtrack. My former professors would have been proud of the elaborate short film that I created for this moment that could not have taken more than a few seconds in real life. I kept playing it on a loop in my head until it finally lulled me into a pleasant sleep.

The following morning, I woke up refreshed and happy, but as is many times the case, the dawn brought with it a sense of reality and my romantic musings of only a few hours ago were quickly replaced with the preparations for a new day. I knew that I would not see Lina until our next class and that was still a week away. Although a disappointing fact for me in and of itself, it would serve for the romantic moment between us to fade, provided there had been a romantic moment between us and not only a passing fancy on my part. Lina would simply be an insanely hot girl who happened to be taking my class. It was not the first time, and it would not be the last.

Not particularly happy, but sufficiently satisfied with my mature and practical assessment of the situation, I went about my day as usual. I had walk-in office hours on Tuesday afternoons until 4.00 p.m. After meeting with a few students, I was getting ready to leave when I received a phone call.

"Hi, Professor Victor. It's Lina Velasquez from your Media Aesthetics class."

This was a little strange. First, she had addressed me by title and first name as if we were in a period romance novel. Second, she had identified herself by given name, surname, and course affiliation, as if I needed the additional clarification to know who she was. Was she establishing boundaries after the previous night's event? Once again, I use the term event loosely. Perhaps I was awarding it hidden meanings and interpretations that it did not merit. My answer was non-committal.

"Hello, Lina."

"I know I didn't make an appointment in advance, but would you be able to see me at 4.30 p.m. today?"

I did not mention either the fact that you did not need an appointment for walk-in office hours, or that my office hours ended at 4.00 p.m.

"Sure," I answered.

"*Great,*" Lina replied. "See you then."

And that was the end of it.

The half hour I waited for her felt like a year. I scolded myself every few minutes for creating drama without any real reason for doing so. After all, there was nothing particularly earth-shattering about a student coming to see a professor in his office. 4.30 p.m. arrived, and, punctual as a Swiss watch, Lina was gently knocking on my door in all her sexy splendor. She was dressed all in blue with tight jeans and a long sweater that hugged her curves. I motioned for her to take a seat. Not wishing to overanalyze anything, I simply asked, "What can I help you with today?"

She seemed a bit nervous and started, "Well, you can probably tell by now that I'm a very passionate person…"

These first few words made me nervous, but I remained expressionless and simply looked at her.

"*…And sometimes I express myself in ways that I probably shouldn't…*"

At this point the combination of anxiety and excitement was almost too much for me to bear, so I casually crossed my leg and slightly inclined my head as a sign of increased attention.

"*…But it's hard for me to control myself and right now, the passion that is dominating my life…*"

I cannot swear it, but I think a slight sound may have escaped from my throat, whether it expressed agony or joy, I could no longer tell.

"*…Is radio.*"

She finished the sentence and looked at me expectantly.

What the fuck is this woman talking about? I exclaimed loudly inside my brain, but luckily, my proper breeding kicked in.

"I'm not sure I understand, Lina. What is it that you need from me?"

She seemed to relax at the question and proceeded to explain that although she had always been interested in television, she had recently acquired a fiery passion for radio and that it was now her dream to become an on-air radio personality. She was taking an Audio Production class and as an assignment she had to conduct an interview that was scheduled for tonight. She had been lucky enough to secure a well-known, local radio DJ and she was nervous about committing any faux pas during the process.

My mind had imagined a million directions in which our conversation could have gone, but I was not prepared for something so… academic.

"Have you talked to your audio professor about it?" I asked, not knowing what else to say.

She said she had, but that she wanted my opinion because she considered me to be very eloquent when speaking and elegant in my manner. Without a doubt, eloquence and elegance were wonderful traits to be complimented on, and I was flattered by her statements, but in truth, I felt disappointed that the encounter had not taken a more personal turn.

Resigned to the fact that it was indeed ridiculous for me to assume that Lina and I had personal issues to deal with in the first place, I gave her some perfunctory advice about firm handshakes, eye contact and not fawning over celebrities, regardless of their status. I stood up, abruptly ending our meeting, and said, "Well, good luck. Let me know how it goes."

Lina stood up as well and replied, "I definitely will. Thank you so much for the advice. I really appreciate you taking the time to meet with me."

Uttering these words, her beautiful feline eyes opened wide, and she gave me such a look of admiration, adoration and, dare I say, passion, that I was once again entranced. I put my hand gently on her waist and leaned in toward her without realizing what I was doing. As if attracted by an invisible magnet, she lifted her face toward mine, and our lips met in the most incredible kiss that I had ever had in my life. It was one of those deep, passionate kisses that you feel reverberating in the very core of your being. It seemed to last forever, and when we finally disengaged, it was like we were still floating in the clouds. The look of surprised happiness on her face was priceless, and I can remember it even now. Despite everything that happened afterward between us, I still remember that moment with fondness and nostalgia.

Unfortunately, as all good things must eventually come to an end, so it had to be with this. As early as the following evening, I was already doubting my judgement in pursuing this situation any further. It was now Wednesday evening, and it was to be our first official date. We drove into Manhattan, had a romantic candlelight dinner, and held hands like a couple of teenagers in love. When it came time for our goodnight kiss, I was hoping for an encore of the previous day, but what I got was something vastly different. If the first kiss had made me fly, the second one set me on fire. It was passionate as well, but this time around, it was much more aggressive and very sexually charged. She held on tightly to my long hair and pressed her body to mine as if she had no intention of ever letting go. In the trembling of her body,

I sensed a powerful combination of fear, desperation and overwhelming desire that made it seem that she not only wanted to devour my body but claim my soul as well. It is important to remember that it had been less than forty-eight hours since I had first given her a ride home. I cannot say that I did not enjoy this intensity of feeling as it incited the pleasure in all my senses, but it also made me feel uneasy. There was trouble in paradise.

Once again, ignoring all the signs that screamed for me to hit the brakes on this runaway train of conflicting emotions, I met Lina's mother the following evening, which was a Thursday, and introduced her as my girlfriend to Sal on Friday. The weekend began on Saturday morning by Lina and I declaring over the phone to one another that our situation would be a love story for the ages, followed by our first verbal argument, also via phone, on Saturday night and our subsequent break-up on Sunday. The love story for the ages had lasted less than a week.

Even the most observant of people may have missed the fact that Lina and I did not spend Saturday together. She had joked about giving me permission to spend the day with Sal. In hindsight, it seems that she was not joking at all.

"Great catch, man!" Sal laughed, attacking a bucket of Kentucky Fried Chicken in my basement. "She is definitely a hottie. Kind of like if Jessica Alba and Shakira had a daughter together."

Sal would always come up with the most unique and unexpected phrases. "But what's with the girlfriend title? Didn't you just bang her for the first time a few days ago? Seems like you're jumping the gun on this one."

"I haven't banged her yet, as you so eloquently put it. We've just spent a lot of time together."

"No kidding?" he asked and then, as if considering whether

61

to believe me or not, he added, "What? Are you saving yourself for marriage?"

This was accompanied by a loud, vulgar laugh displaying a mouthful of fried chicken which made me cringe and wonder how our friendship had survived so many years with our wildly different personalities.

"You know me better than that, Sally. Guys like us have way too much love to give out, and we can't spend it all in the same place."

It was the right answer for the current environment of primitive male bonding, and it saved me from ever having to admit to Sal that I *had* allowed my mind to wander in the direction of nuptial bliss when it came to Lina. Sal and I spent the day together and we had a blast. We played pool at my house, then went to the local arcade where we commandeered the Mortal Kombat game, much to the disappointment of a group of teenagers that did not dare say anything to a couple of grown men shouting like maniacs every time we ran out of lives. We then played basketball and flirted with a few of the local girls at the park while exchanging contact information. Finally, we headed back to my house with an ice-cold six-pack of Heineken and a piping hot Meat Lovers pizza from Domino's. We settled in to binge-watch Prison Break when I noticed my cell phone was vibrating on one of the end tables. I flipped it open and saw the message *19 missed calls* on the screen.

"What the…" I started to say but was interrupted by Sal.

"Vic! Come on. We're like ten episodes behind. Let's see what new tricks our resident genius, Michael Scofield has up his sleeve."

I checked the phone again and saw that sixteen of the nineteen calls had been made by Lina., two were from Riverdale

University, and the other one was from one of the girls I had met at the park. I decided that I would deal with Riverdale during work hours, and probably wait a couple of days to get back to the new girl, but the multiple calls from Lina gave me a bad feeling. There were no actual texts or voicemails, so it could not be an emergency. I had last talked to her at noon, and it was now 8.00 p.m. I scrolled through the time stamps and saw that she had called me every half hour for the last eight hours. I decided that I would call her at 10.00 p.m. so Sal and I could get at least a couple of episodes in, but the truth is that it was hard for me to focus, especially because the phone vibrated four more times during the program. I pretended not to notice and did not answer even though I knew perfectly well who it was. Sal just looked at me through the corner of his eye without saying a word. He also knew what was going on, but, sensing my discomfort, decided to let it go as only a true friend does.

At almost midnight, Sal declared loudly that he was wiped out and was hitting the sack. "Must be getting old. It's not even tomorrow yet."

With that, he started rearranging the cushions on the sofa, so that he could convert it into a bed. Subtle and classy as always, he did not bother asking if he could crash for the night. He just assumed he could. This was my cue to go upstairs to my own bedroom.

To describe in detail what I was feeling at that moment would be quite a blow to my masculinity, but, suffice it to say, the overwhelming sentiment was an irrational sense of fear. Ridiculous as it sounds, I was afraid to face my girlfriend of less than a week on the phone. Embarrassed at my pathetic emotional state, I decided to get it over with, and use a casual tone as my weapon of choice. My plan was not successful.

"Hey, baby. Just wanted to send you a good night kiss before turning in."

"Where were you?"

"What do you mean?"

"Do you know what time it is?"

"I know it's a bit late, but I thought it might still be OK to call."

"I haven't heard from you all day."

"Not true. We spoke this morning, and we are speaking now."

Silence.

"You knew I was spending the day with Sal. We talked about it."

Silence.

"Come on. What's wrong? Talk to me."

I had frequently heard the saying hell hath no fury like a woman scorned but to be honest, I would have probably been better off opening the gates of hell. The intensity of the recriminations launched at me defied any logic.

"Why you gotta be like dat? How you gonna treat yo' boo like she some back-up ho while you out scoping the field like some playa? A real man don't treat his bitch like that!"

I was stunned into silence. I knew about Lina's background, but I was not prepared for the full force of the ghetto to accompany her tirade. She went on in the same vein for a while until she abruptly seemed to realize how she was speaking and took a deep breath to try to control herself. Then, consciously going back to the speech pattern that I had always heard her use.

"I'm sorry, Victor. I don't think it's going to work out between us. Maybe we should just end it now before anyone gets hurt."

"OK," I replied with the tone of someone accepting a coffee refill at a diner instead of the rupture of a romantic relationship.

The truth is that although my simple response may have come across as casual indifference, the tone was the result of my state of shock. I was more than a bit confused as to what had just happened. Did she have a split personality, or was it just a matter of her feelings getting the better of her? It was certainly not uncommon for individuals to lapse back into forgotten speech patterns in times of heightened emotion, but what I had heard seemed more like an audiobook version of 'The Exorcist.' Lina not only sounded angry, she sounded like she was under some sort of demonic possession. Once the evil spirit of the ghetto was expelled from her body, she went back to being a scholarship student at Riverdale University. Making light of the situation with my socially insensitive and politically incorrect internal jokes made me feel better. I had dodged a bullet, and now I could go on with my life. That, in any event, is what I told myself.

The following day was basically uneventful. It was a cool, crisp Sunday, and I spent most of the day outdoors jogging and riding my bicycle. I received a few flirty, appreciative glances from fellow joggers on the trail, but other than smiling back out of politeness, I was back to my shy, unsociable self. It was like the previous week with Lina had never even happened. It seemed more like an extended dream, and now I was awake again. I returned refreshed, both physically and mentally, spent a quiet evening at home, and calmly accepted the fact that my relationship with Lina had ended – except it had not.

The next day it was Monday again, and I assumed that due to recent events, Lina would be absent from class, at least that was my hope. I knew she was too responsible a student to drop a class in mid-November, but I figured she might take a day to calm down, and then just deal with the handful of classes left in the semester. I was wrong.

She showed up in all her voluptuous glory to class. I have mentioned on several occasions how insanely hot this woman was, but that evening she was exuding a sexuality that made me instantly regret our break-up. Lina had on a red and black leather outfit that was more appropriate for a music video than a classroom. As usual, it hugged every curve of her amazingly toned body. The top offered a view of her cleavage that made it hard for me to concentrate on anything else. Once she had made her grand entrance, and caused a stir among the students, she demurely put on a black denim jacket and sat down.

I was certainly not prepared for the flood of feelings that came rushing back into my body and mind. I tried my best to feign indifference during the lecture, but I failed miserably. Several male students tried to approach her that evening during the break, but she only had eyes for me. Every time our gazes met, she would either be staring at me with love and admiration or otherwise unabashed sexual desire. This back and forth between us did not escape the students. There were giggles, murmurs, and whispers which I tried to ignore, again, failing at every opportunity.

When the class was finally over, and students started exiting the classroom, I got a few *'Enjoy your night, Professor Steiner,'* with meaningful smirks, especially from the male students. Some of the female students looked offended, and either offered icy farewells or left without saying anything to me at all, shooting daggers at Lina with their eyes as they left. Still others, both male and female, looked at me with an expression which at the time did not register, but in hindsight, I would equate with how you view someone who is about to fall, but you are powerless to stop it.

Lina approached me with a cautious but calculated step which I assumed was her way of making me be the one to initiate dialogue. I did not take the bait.

"Have a good night," I said to no one in particular, as there were still a few students mulling about. "Don't forget that your research papers are due after Thanksgiving break," I reminded them as I started leaving.

"Professor Steiner..." Lina started to say with a not-quite-steady voice.

"Yes?" I answered, trying desperately to avoid eye contact at all costs.

"Do you have a minute? I'd like to run something by you... about my research paper."

Walk away. No, run away. In fact, run for your life. Do not look back. Save yourself. All these thoughts screamed loudly inside my brain.

"It's late," I said bravely. "If you stop by during my office hours..." I continued, emboldened by my unexpected willpower.

"Please..." she said, touching my forearm and forcing me to look at her. There they were, those beautifully hypnotic cat-like eyes, a strange paradox of angel and succubus, offering me both heaven and hell with their alluring trance.

"Let's go to my office," I replied, utterly vanquished. So much for willpower.

From an intellectual perspective, I knew, even back then, that I would live to regret my weakness. I had escaped unscathed from the first round, and now I was foolishly tempting my luck. By the time we had reached my office, the temptress was gone, and the polite college student had returned. It is amazing how the mind can trick itself into believing what the heart wants it to. I was listening to a woman who looked like she had just stepped out of a S&M magazine spread, but within minutes I viewed her as a damsel in distress that needed rescuing.

She explained how her insane jealousy was really a lack of confidence in herself, and her inability to keep a man by her side. Although probably true in behavioral terms, I personally found it hard to believe that such an attractive woman would have this problem, but I lent a sympathetic ear, nonetheless. She confessed that our relationship, short as it had been, went far beyond physical attraction, and that she was deeply and hopelessly in love with me. She admitted that men were constantly approaching her, a fact that I had myself witnessed on several occasions, but that she only wanted me. She had found the love of her life, and she refused to let me go. As she spoke, she allowed her tears to flow freely, and, as my mirror neurons were in full swing, we were soon both crying in each other's arms.

With such a heightened state of emotions, the reconciliation between us was all but inevitable. It started with a slow, deliberate, exploratory kiss, reminiscent of the first one we had shared less than a week ago. As it increased in intensity, it soon became a frenzied session of passionate lovemaking. I felt such a range of emotions that it scared me, but I was too vested in the moment to think clearly. Lina would switch from sweet and submissive one moment, to aggressive and dominant the next. The pleasure I felt was so great that I felt I could easily have died at that moment without regrets. As these dangerous thoughts were taking control of me, I felt like I was losing my soul.

So began the vicious cycle of the most toxic relationship I ever experienced in my life. Genuine moments of tenderness and love, followed by hysterical arguments, stemming from irrational jealousy on both our parts, culminating in aggressive bouts of exhausting sex. Lather. Rinse. Repeat. Although it felt like an eternity, our relationship lasted only a few weeks. By the time the Christmas break came along, we had called it quits for good.

Of the many unfortunate consequences that result from giving in to an all-consuming passion, one of the most damaging is that the sense of priorities is lost, and many times the problems created cannot be repaired. After almost twelve years at Riverdale University, with the promise of all-but-guaranteed tenure at my fingertips, I failed to show up for my review. The previous night had been one of my reconciliation sessions with Lina, and I had simply slept through the review appointment. When I realized what had happened, it was already too late. No number of apologies were enough to make amends. The university had taken my absence as a sign of unforgivable disrespect, and I had been irrevocably denied tenure.

This may not seem particularly tragic to most people. After all, why should anyone expect to secure lifetime employment anywhere, especially before turning thirty? I agree. I still had four decades of work ahead of me, and this was certainly not the end of my career. What really infuriated me was to let a golden opportunity slip through my fingers in such a ridiculous way. On top of that, Riverdale University encouraged all faculty that had been denied tenure to explore other opportunities during the following semester. This was basically code for *find another job* as no faculty that had been denied tenure at Riverdale had lasted more than an additional semester afterwards at the university. The additional semester basically acted as a temporary safety net while new employment was found. If anyone tried to extend his time, Riverdale University would simply find a reason, legitimate or not, why the individual was not a good match for the core values of the institution and, as it was an at-will employer, had no real legal ramifications to worry about.

I had been there long enough to know the drill, so I requested to do a semester abroad for my remaining time at Riverdale. Although an unusual request, the university granted it. I guess they figured I had earned it and would be more likely to leave quietly if given this concession. Truthfully, I had no intention of challenging the decision. In a way, I embraced it, as it would give me the opportunity to start fresh somewhere else and leave the craziness of the past few weeks behind me.

As it turns out, my final semester at Riverdale University promised to be an exciting one. I would be teaching Film and Television at a university in Mumbai and producing a series of documentaries that would allow me to travel around India, all expenses paid. Not too bad for someone a few months away from unemployment.

I shared the news with my parents and, in fact, spent the entire holiday break with them. They must have sensed that I was going through a difficult moment and decided to put their international philanthropy on hold for my benefit. Although it was not really a common occurrence with them, I appreciated the gesture and fully enjoyed our time together. I also took the opportunity to patch things up with Sal. As a true friend, he acted as if nothing had happened, and our fraternal ties were quickly restored. Despite all the preceding drama, Lina and I had ended our relationship on cordial terms, so all in all, I was in a good place. All things considered; I was happier than I had been in a long time.

My time in India allowed me to gain a lot of perspective on what I wanted to do with my life. When I was denied tenure, my first thought had been that I had lost several years that I would never get back, but, as time went by, I realized that every cloud has a silver lining. Had I become a tenured professor, I would have felt obligated to stay at Riverdale University forever, but the more time I spent in the field producing the series of documentaries that my semester abroad required, the more I understood that this is what I wanted to dedicate my life to. I had just turned thirty, and I had my whole life ahead of me.

As if this realization were not reward enough, I met my future business partner and wife, Priya. She was a doctoral student in London and was also spending a semester abroad doing research for her dissertation. Being of Indian descent, for her, this was both a study in sociology and an exploration of her ancestral roots. To say that my relationship with Priya was different from my relationship with Lina would be the understatement of the century. We met in New Delhi, at an international conference of Media, Culture, and Communication. We exchanged contact information, became first casual acquaintances, then good friends, eventually fell in love and were married five years later. We settled in London, set up our own production house, and traveled around the world showcasing our work at various venues.

So, in the end, everything turned out well and no one was hurt, right? Afraid not. It had been ten years since my relationship with Lina had ended. I would occasionally remember our time together and had perhaps mentioned her a couple of times in passing to my wife, without offering any specific details. Priya and I had decided early on in our relationship that we would leave our past lovers in the past as talking in depth about them would not provide any benefit to our life as a married couple. My fortieth birthday was coming up and Priya was pulling out all the stops. In direct contrast to my personality, she was a social butterfly. Everyone that encountered her was impressed by her beauty, grace, and good taste. She had organized a formal dinner at a local club near our home, and as we were now something of an established celebrity couple in our field, the guest list was as distinguished as it could be for the occasion. This type of setting made me extremely uncomfortable, and I told her so, but she refused to let me have my way, which would have consisted in a quiet afternoon at home with our twin baby daughters, Jana and Jaya.

"You only turn forty once, sweetheart," she said to me, flashing her beautiful black eyes and flipping back her jet-black tresses.

In a classy black dress, with gold earrings and matching necklace, she had nothing to envy any A-list Bollywood actress. In turn, I felt like a prisoner in a straitjacket in my tuxedo, but a passionate kiss, and the look of genuine love in Priya's eyes made it all worthwhile.

Many times in life, it is at the moments when we feel the safest that we are the most vulnerable. Who would have imagined that something that had long ago been buried as a distant memory would suddenly gain a new lifeforce so strong that it would leave only destruction and misery in its path? I cannot remember all the specific details. Perhaps I simply choose not to remember them, but the consequences of what happened the evening of my birthday party dinner, I will never be able to escape.

As my wife, beautiful and elegant as always, was making a toast in my honor, a long-unheard voice resounded in the back of the rented hall.

"I would like to make a toast too!"

There she was, standing in all her erotic sensuality, wrapped in a short, sexy black dress that belonged more at a dance club than at a formal dinner event, nervously clutching a small purse in her hands. Both the interruption and her physique and demeanor turned every single head in the room. I was so shocked that I was unable to utter a single word. Lina looked amazing. As she walked closer to me, I could tell that she had made it a priority to stay in excellent shape. However, her face was almost unrecognizable. Although still strikingly beautiful, she looked like a woman in her late fifties, and not someone barely in her thirties. Her features were highlighted by lines that denoted anger and bitterness and the gorgeous, feline eyes that had been the cause of many sleepless nights for me, had lost their shine, and offered only hatred as she seemed to stare right into my soul.

"What are you doing here?" I finally asked stupidly.

"Me?" she asked with a quivering voice and flaring nostrils. "I'm here to wish you a happy birthday, Professor Steiner. After all, I am your most cherished student, don't you remember?"

This was all said with the cadence of the scholarship student I remembered well. Although a stranger to the crowd, it was not difficult to put two and two together. Our guests were all well-educated people, and although ignorant of the details, were able to figure out what was going on.

One of Priya's former professors, was the first to interfere.

"Madame, perhaps if you care to step outside…"

Lina turned toward him savagely.

"Madame? I ain't no madame. I'm just some hoochie from the Bronx, or didn't Victor tell you?"

This caused some murmurs and whispers throughout the guests and made me very uneasy as it reminded me of the first time she had blown up at me years ago. The long-dormant demon of the ghetto was rearing its ugly head again. This last thought made me giggle nervously, which not only earned me a hard, incredulous stare from my wife, but fueled Lina's wrath tenfold.

"You think that funny? You figure, let me have some fun and slum it with a skank from the hood, rip her heart out, and then throw her away, so I can happily ever after with some Bollywood bitch?" she screamed, gesturing toward Priya, who to her credit, although visibly upset, kept her composure in a most dignified manner.

Another guest, a young man who was the main camera operator on our overseas shoots, approached Lina.

"Please miss, calm down."

This show of politeness seemed to anger her even more, and she pulled a gun from her purse.

"Back off!" she yelled.

A few people started moving toward the exits quietly, but then Lina raised the gun over her head and fired twice into the chandelier above. The report of the shots, and the resulting rain of shards of crystal caused pandemonium. Guests were running in every direction, knocking over tables, and trampling each other in their efforts to escape. Lina ignored the people that flanked her on either side trying to reach the exits but was merciless with anyone who stood between her and me. The first victim was one of Priya's cousins. She had just graduated high school and was planning to attend college in the United States in the fall. A bullet between the eyes stopped that plan it its tracks. Two servers also met their doom when they crashed into each other trying to flee and inadvertently blocked Lina's path toward me. Two more shots. Two more lives extinguished. Lina kept walking toward me with the determination of a she-wolf. As our table faced a wall, we had nowhere to go, so I instinctually grabbed hold of Priya, and shielded her with my body.

"Oh, that's so sweet!" intoned Lina psychotically. "What a

fucking gentleman. Too bad this brown whore won't live much longer to enjoy you."

She kept trying to come around me, and point her gun directly at Priya, but I kept up with her movements, so she could not get a clear shot without hitting me.

At this point, my head was swimming. I believe the fact that she did not want to shoot me is what ultimately saved my life, but I ended up paying a high price, nonetheless. I picked up a nearby knife and pointed it at Lina, trying unsuccessfully to keep my voice steady.

"Lina. Please put the gun down. I don't want to hurt you."

Lina seemed surprised that I had a weapon of my own and lapsed back into her honor roll student speech.

"You don't want to hurt me, Victor? But you already hurt me. I gave myself to you mind, body and soul, and you just left me as if nothing had ever happened between us."

With these words she started crying, and lowered the gun, placing it on the table. I should have gone for the gun then and there, but Lina sank to the floor, and started sobbing uncontrollably as her body trembled. Instead, I motioned to Priya to get the gun and mouthed the word *police* while I cautiously approached the miserable woman on the floor with the intention of getting her back on her feet. Priya looked at me angrily, but started to comply when suddenly, the loud wailing of sirens was heard on the street. Thankfully, someone had already called the police, but unfortunately, the sound brought Lina back to reality, and she went for the gun just as Priya was reaching for it.

They arrived at the same time, but Lina was quicker with her hands. She pointed the gun directly at Priya's chest and pulled the trigger. Nothing. She pulled it again. Nothing. I did not realize it at the time, but the cartridge had been spent. Two bullets for the chandelier. One bullet for each of the three victims. Five total. Exasperated at her lack of success, she threw the gun aside, picked up a nearby knife and started making slashing motions toward Priya. I had a knife as well, but the idea of stabbing someone made me sick to the stomach, so I threw it aside and rushed at Lina with the intention of tackling her. She saw me coming, and once again, was quick to react.

The slashing motions were now directed toward me, but I could tell from the look in her eyes that she was just putting on a show because she really did not want to physically harm me. Emboldened by this certainty in my mind, I did not back down. Priya then seized the opportunity to grab hold of a bottle of wine and threw it at Lina with all her might. Unfortunately, good aim was not one of my wife's qualities, and she missed the target completely.

However, the intent itself enraged Lina, so she attacked my wife mercilessly slashing at her face and arms. Priya tried to defend herself, but the results of that fateful evening ended up scarring her for life, both physically and emotionally. Filled with horror and rage, I tackled Lina with the force of a linebacker, and pinned her to the ground. She struggled like a wild animal, but I was too strong for her, or so I thought. She had dropped the knife in the scuffle, so I foolishly relaxed my grip on her. Terrible mistake. She managed to knee me in the groin, and then my years of high school and college football became worthless. As I howled in pain, I saw my wife in the corner crying hysterically, her beautiful face covered by a veil of blood.

"Priya!" I cried helplessly with the little air I could muster.

Apparently, it was the wrong thing to say as Lina landed a savage kick to my throat which lay me flat on my back, and left me gasping more for air, if that was even possible.

Lina then calmly picked up the bloody knife from where it had fallen, put it between her teeth and started crawling toward me on all fours with all the raw sexuality of a Jennifer Lopez music video. She then straddled me and made sure that I was a prisoner between her powerful knees and thighs. If I had not been so terrified, I would have fancied myself the protagonist in a gothic horror porn fantasy.

If I had been able to speak, I would have cried out for help, but all that escaped my lips was a moan. Lina grossly misinterpreted my reaction and taking the knife out of her mouth started rubbing against me with her body.

"Mmmmmm," she cooed. "You like that, don't you? Just like old times."

This woman was obviously insane. Why did I get involved with her in the first place? I knew from the very first moment I saw her that she would be trouble. Granted, I never expected this level of insanity, but I should have known better. It would have been more prudent to put the brakes on our relationship from the very beginning. This could have been prevented. Would have. Should have. Could have. What a mess. Suddenly my thoughts were interrupted by a crisp, clear, commanding male voice.

"Miss, put down the knife. I will not ask you again."

Again? I asked myself dumbly. *When did you ask the first time?*

The police report would later confirm that the officers had ordered Lina to put down the weapon three times. Not that this was particularly threatening, considering the police force in London does not carry firearms. Lina looked at me with big, sad eyes. Even with the extreme changes in her face, and the horrifying situation we found ourselves in, she still looked gorgeous. She pressed the tip of the knife to the middle of my chest. I closed my eyed accepting my fate. I was too paralyzed with fear to move a muscle. She gently opened my eyes, and tenderly caressed my face saying in the sweetest of voices, "Don't worry, baby. I always knew we would end up together in the end."

She then softly kissed my lips which either would not, or simply could not, respond to her touch, and let out a long, dramatic sigh. Then, quick as lightning, she reversed the position of the knife with the blade pointing at her own chest and thrust her chest with full force on top of mine. The voice I had lost came back with a vengeance as I let out a scream. Both my wife and the police later reported thinking I was the one who had been penetrated by the knife. With the last gasps of her dying breath, Lina declared her love for me for the final time.

"I love you, Victor," she said through a mouth already filling with blood. "I always will."

She clutched me tightly and desperately as she would always do after our sessions of passionate lovemaking for a moment, then went limp, and died.

It has been almost two years since the events of that horrible day. Priya and I are still married, but I cannot honestly say that we are together. Things will never be the same between us. I often see her staring at her reflection in the mirror and sadly tracing her fingers over her scars. Although we paid for the best plastic surgeons in England, they were not able to fully restore the regal beauty she was so proud of. Of course, the emotional scars run much deeper. We both have frequent nightmares that feature Lina and wake up screaming and drenched in sweat. At first, we would try to comfort each other but after a while, we just accepted it as routine, and now simply ignore one another when it happens.

Priya has never openly accused me of being responsible for what happened, but the resentment is there. She tries to hide it, but not very successfully, especially when looking in the mirror. Our once amazing communication has dwindled in the last couple of years as well, and our level of intimacy is practically non-existent.

Our business has also suffered. Clients tend to stay away from people directly involved in such a high-profile story that was the talk of London for several weeks, and eventually made its way back to New York. I did not feel like I could go back to Riverdale and face everyone, but London did not feel like home anymore either. Priya was adamant about staying in London, so that was another point of contention between us.

I do not feel our marriage will last much longer. The main reason we stay together is for our daughters' sakes. There are some damages that are so profound that, even with the best of intentions, they can never be repaired. All of this could have been avoided if I had followed my gut instinct from the beginning. For all those that claim that first impressions should be discarded as biased opinions that have no foundation in truth, I hope that you will view my story as a cautionary tale. First impressions may be wrong many times, but when they are right, they can also spell the difference between life and death.

Overdue Apology

Throughout the ages, man has studied human emotion extensively. Although there exists a plethora of scientific theories connecting nerve endings to chemical reactions in the brain, and environmental agents to sensory perceptions, there is no one, true formulaic explanation to justify the phenomenon surrounding human emotions, especially those that come suddenly and with great force.

Jason Hanson experienced such an emotion when he walked into the conference room, and saw Konrad Forest sitting next to his boss on the second day of the new year. The feeling was like red-hot coals had been placed in his throat and were slowly sliding down the delicate lining of his stomach. Jason was afraid. No, that is not quite true. He was terrified. It was ridiculous. He had no reason to feel this way. They were both grown men, and at least twenty years had passed since they had last seen each other. Konrad could not still be angry, could he?

"How good of you to grace us with your presence, Hanson. You're only forty minutes late."

Jason was surprised out of his earlier thoughts. He looked at his watch, and suddenly found that he had forgotten how to tell time. Was the large hand the minutes and the small hand the hours, or was it the other way around? Jason seemed to struggle with the concept, and then looked up with a dumb expression on his face.

The man he was looking at was Mr. Thorpe; an obese, red-faced Texan that was pushing seventy and still had an enviable mane of long, silver hair. He had been Jason's boss for the past five years, and the company president for close to two decades. He was extremely loud and obnoxious and had a lion's roar of a laugh that would make anything near him shiver and shake, including his enormous belly. Jason could not comprehend how such a man had been awarded the presidency of an advertising agency. He knew that schmoozing was an important part of the industry, but Thorpe was downright vulgar. He cursed freely, regardless of the setting, and had no problem hitting on his employees' wives and girlfriends whenever he saw an opportunity. On top of everything else, he wore a cowboy hat and string tie to work, although he had not lived in his native Texas for over thirty years after coming to New York in his late thirties. Jason could not trust anyone who would so openly refuse to adapt to the place he was living in.

Of course, Jason had first-hand experience with adaptation. He had been born Yazin Hansur. His family had immigrated to the United States when he was a child, barely escaping being massacred by rebels in their native country. Ever since he was a small boy, he had been embarrassed by his family and background, and had done everything in his power to conceal them. As soon as he had seen the opportunity, he had left his parents' house in Jackson Heights, and moved to a tiny studio apartment in Astoria. He was only a short subway ride away from his family, but the times he had visited them since leaving could be counted on both hands, probably with fingers left over.

But, for anyone who cared to inquire, he had always been Jason Hanson from Queens. His parents had retired to Honolulu, and, since it was so far away, he could not visit them often. Of course, not often really meant never since Jason had never been even remotely close to Hawaii in his life. In fact, the only time he ever left Queens was to go to work at *Empire Advertising* in Manhattan.

"Well, don't just stand there looking like a jackass! What do you want, a fucking invitation?" Thorpe barked at him.

"No, sir. I just..." Jason began meekly.

"Never mind. Come on in. You look like my old cow, Betsy, waiting for her morning tit-squeezing."

At this, Thorpe burst out laughing as spittle flew out of his mouth. Most of the people in the conference room took it as a cue, and joined in heartily, ignoring the disgusting display of inappropriate behavior by their boss. Jason quickly glanced at Konrad, who was one of the few people not laughing. He only had the faint trace of a smile playing about his lips.

The asshole is probably enjoying this more than anyone else, Jason thought sourly. By now, his initial fear had been replaced by embarrassment. He walked in with flushed cheeks, and took the seat to the left of Konrad, which was the only one available. As he sat down, Konrad gave him a friendly smile, and then looked away before seeing the bitter scowl returned by Jason.

The laughter in the conference room finally ended, and when everybody had settled down, Thorpe began speaking again. He could have just as easily brought the room to order with a single word but seemed to enjoy Jason's public humiliation too much to do such a thing.

"Well, now, listen up you lazy sons of bitches. We got us a brand-spanking-new European import here, Mr. Konrad Forest from Germany..." He paused for a moment as if considering the information. "Or is it Denmark?"

Konrad smiled politely. "It's actually both, sir. I've been going back and forth between countries for the past ten years."

"So you have."

Thorpe waved his hands dismissively as if warding off an annoying fly. He had apparently noticed the longing stares of the female employees in the conference room as Konrad spoke in his deep, rich baritone. Thorpe always liked being the center of attention and this pretty boy was taking that away from him.

"So, what are you, German or Dutch?" Thorpe continued, not without a slight trace of jealousy in his voice.

Konrad surveyed the room quickly as if deciding whether to answer or not. Jason once again observed the ever-so-slight smile form on Konrad's lips before he spoke.

"I'm Canadian, Mr. Thorpe..." He then paused for a moment. "...And I think you mean Danish, sir."

"What?" asked Thorpe, genuinely puzzled.

"Dutch people are from the Netherlands. Danish people are from Denmark."

Thorpe grew redder than he normally was. Sweat began forming on his pudgy face, and he could feel his undershirt beginning to stick uncomfortably to his skin. The room was in total silence. All the attendees were frozen in their seats. No one had ever dared call Thorpe out on any of his mistakes, never mind in a room full of people. *Game over*, Jason thought maliciously to himself. It was for the best. He did not like the idea of having to work with Konrad one bit. It did not matter that everything had happened so many years ago.

Jason's thoughts were interrupted by a high wheezing sound coming from Thorpe's chest. At first, Jason thought that the old man was going to have a heart attack. He then realized that it was just the beginning of Thorpe's characteristic bray of vulgar laughter. Just like before, everyone in the conference room started to join in when they felt it was safe. The king has laughed.

Jason thought to himself in disgust, *These people were truly pathetic.* He turned to look at Konrad, and once again there was only the slightest trace of a smile on his face. Konrad and Jason were the only two people in the room that were not laughing this time.

The meeting took the customary, unnecessary three hours that it did every Monday morning. There was more talk of the holiday activities than anything related to work. Through it all, Jason watched Konrad closely, who in turn would listen attentively to whomever was speaking. Jason began to feel something dangerously close to hatred toward the new man on the team. His manner denoted class, but he did not seem the least bit stiff. He was completely clean-cut, not a single hair out of place. His long, wavy, black hair was tied back in a perfectly formed ponytail. He was well-built, and it seemed that his clothing was custom-made to fit the contours of his body. He had piercing, black eyes behind lightly tinted glasses that also partially covered a small, white scar above his right eye. Jason had not thought about that scar in a long time, perhaps because he had never actually seen it healed. That time, they had simply gone too far.

It was a rainy, Friday afternoon in Queens. Jackson Heights Junior High School was just about closed for the winter holidays. The only people left were the boys on the hockey team, who were also in charge of cleaning up, and putting away equipment at the After School Center. The director, Mr. Kingsley, was always the one to lock up, but today he had had to leave early because his elderly mother had fallen down the stairs and had to be rushed to the hospital. Earlier that afternoon, he had called two of the boys to his office.

"Sit down, boys," Kingsley had said.

Konrad and Yazin had done as they were told.

"Now I'm going to ask you boys for a big favor. My mom took a nasty spill down the stairs. I have to go to the hospital and be with her. Konrad, I am going to give you the keys to the center. I want you to lock up today. When you come back from the break, before reporting to homeroom, come to my office, and return the keys to me. Nobody needs to know about this, boys. It'll be our little deal, OK?"

He looked directly at Yazin when he said this last part. Kingsley knew he could trust Konrad. He was an Honor Roll student and an all-around well-educated and pleasant boy. At the same time, he did not like Yazin at all, and he certainly did not trust him. He was a foul-mouthed punk and a troublemaker. However, Kingsley was of the mentality that it was important to have some of the bad kids on your side. If you only stuck to the goody-two-shoes, you would be branded as a loser. That is why he had chosen Yazin to help at the After School Center, and that is why he had called him in with Konrad this afternoon. It was his security policy. Unfortunately, Kingsley's lack of good judgement would have profoundly serious consequences.

Kingsley reiterated how important it was to keep this arrangement secret to the boys, and then left them alone. Konrad felt extremely uncomfortable, not to mention a little bit afraid. He did not like the idea of being left alone with the tough hockey crowd. Although he was on the hockey team himself, he was relentlessly bullied by the other players. They would taunt him, and jeer at him, and, on more than one occasion, they would physically hurt him. As horrible as it is to admit, Konrad was an easy target. At thirteen, he was almost six feet tall, but so skinny it appeared a gentle wind could break him in half. Acne had not been kind to him, and he wore thick glasses. He also had braces and because he was constantly biting his nails due to nervousness and anxiety, his fingertips looked like something out of an old horror movie. If anyone had bothered to take a closer look, they would have seen that Konrad was quite a handsome young man, despite his obvious shortcomings. The passing of time would later prove this point, but at Jackson Heights Junior High School, Konrad Forest was the textbook definition of nerd.

Yazin did not waste any time. As soon as Kingsley was gone, he called his buddies over, and started planning what they would do to Konrad. Konrad waited anxiously for it to be closing time, and then started locking up. The other boys did their part, and Konrad did his best to steer clear of them. They would be done in a few minutes. If he had minimal contact with them, perhaps there would not be any trouble.

"Hey, Stringbean, come over here," yelled Leonardo.

He was a fat, Puerto Rican boy with yellow teeth and putrid breath to go along with them.

Konrad turned at the sound of Leonardo's voice. *Not again*, he thought to himself. Instead, he said, "What do you want?" trying to sound tough but doing a poor job at it.

"We need your help, man," Leonardo answered in an almost friendly manner, but Konrad knew better.

Konrad simply turned around and continued locking up.

"Come on, Toothpick! We all want to get out of here," Leonardo said, a little too anxiously.

"What's the hold-up, Leo?" Yazin asked from behind.

He was carrying a mesh bag full of handballs.

"This faggot doesn't want to help out!" Leonardo almost whined.

"Relax, man," Yazin answered and turned to Konrad.

86

"What's the deal, Forest? Kingsley put you in charge."

"Kingsley put us both in charge," Konrad answered, his voice cracking on the last word. This made Leonardo and Yazin howl with laughter. It did not matter that their own voices cracked constantly due to their age. Konrad was always the butt of the joke, and it had to remain that way.

By this time, Konrad could already feel sweat pouring down his forehead and underarms. This situation was going from bad to worse. Why did his voice have to crack at precisely the instant when he was at his most vulnerable? It just was not fair.

"Take it easy, Forest. Nobody's going to hurt you. I need to put these handballs away and I can't reach the container. Neither can Leonardo or Nelson. You're the tallest one," Yazin spoke very slowly as if he were addressing a small child, or perhaps someone with a cognitive disability.

"Use the ladder," Konrad said uneasily.

"The ladder is in Kingsley's office. That's the only key he didn't give you. Come on, man. Help us out, so we can all go home and start our vacation."

Konrad did not know whether the business about the ladder was true, but he decided that he wanted to leave this place as soon as possible, so he went with the boys. He should have realized that he was walking straight into a trap, but he was too nervous to think clearly.

The handball container was on top of an equipment cage in a storage room in the back. It was high, so even Konrad needed to climb on the cage a little to put the balls away because he could not see the top. He secured both his hands on two openings on the cage and then climbed up using two more openings for his feet. He was not too high off the floor, but high enough to hurt himself if he was not careful. When he felt secure enough, he let go of his right hand, and turned toward Yazin and Leonardo.

"OK. Give me the bag now."

The plan was to take hold of the bag, fling it over his head, and hope it landed in the container on top of the cage. What happened next did not take more than thirty seconds, but it seemed like an eternity to all those involved. As Leonardo passed him the bag, Konrad saw something through his peripheral vision. The ladder that was supposedly locked away safely in Kingsley's office was lying lazily on its side under a window in the storage room. Konrad suddenly realized that he had not seen Nelson, one of the other boys in charge of clean-up, in a long time. He turned his head back toward the top of the cage, and the face of a small, blond boy with crazy eyes appeared over the edge.

"What's up, nerd?" he said.

He then cupped his hands under his chin and blew. A thick cloud of white chalk dust flew into Konrad's face and stung his eyes. On instinct, both hands went to his face. The mesh bag hit the floor and the handballs fell out in a series of comical bounces. Konrad fell backwards and lost the balance of his right foot. It would have been better if he had lost his footing altogether because the handballs might have clumsily, but successfully broken his fall. Instead, his left foot remained stuck in the opening, and his leg bent at a painful angle with the weight of the rest of his body. Konrad burst into tears as he dangled from the cage. There was an audible cracking sound, and his sobs quickly escalated to howls of pain. The other boys were frozen with terror. Their little prank had gone terribly wrong, and they had no idea how to remedy the situation.

The first one to react was Yazin.

"Get his foot loose, you fucking idiot!" he yelled at Nelson.

Nelson looked like a terrified small child as he stared dumbly at Yazin.

"I'm out of here," interjected Leonardo, and he ran off without another word.

"Where the fuck are you going?" Yazin screamed after him. "Leo!"

Yazin looked up again, and saw that Nelson was already climbing down the side of the cage.

"What are you doing? Help me get his foot loose," Yazin pleaded.

"You're on your own, man," Nelson said shakily. "I'm not taking the fall for this shit."

"You blew the chalk in his face and made him fall! You're just as guilty as I am!"

"It was your fucking idea. Besides, I'd like to see you prove it. You and Forest were the only ones who were supposed to stay until closing time."

Yazin stared at Nelson in disbelief. Although he was still shaking, Nelson had said this last part in a perfectly calm tone, and in his eyes, Yazin could see that he meant every word. Nelson left the room without even a glance at Konrad, whose face was turning an ugly shade of red due to his upside-down position. Throughout all of this, Konrad was screaming hysterically due to pain, anger and frustration. The pain in his left leg was unbearable, and there was no way he could maneuver his body to get himself free.

Yazin quickly climbed up the cage to try to loosen Konrad's foot. Every time he tried Konrad would howl even louder due to a fresh burst of pain. The fact that he was wriggling around wildly did not make the task any easier for Yazin.

"Shut the fuck up, man. The whole damn neighborhood is

going to hear you," Yazin said in a harsh whisper.

He realized the cruelty of his words but could not help it at that moment. His buddies had left him alone, and he was going to be in more trouble than he had ever been in his life. Konrad just continued crying and screaming. In fact, he was close to passing out. Had Yazin known this, he would not have made the horrible choice he did, but all that he could think about was that an upside-down boy was wailing like a madman, and as soon as someone found them, all the heat would fall on Yazin. Leonardo and Nelson would deny ever being there, and he would probably end up in Juvenile Hall. He jumped down from the cage, grabbed a nearby hockey stick and whacked Konrad on the side of the head. Konrad just hung there dangling like a grotesquely broken doll with blood pouring down the side of his face. Konrad was already passed out when he was hit by the hockey stick, but Yazin's state of anxiety had convinced him that he had been hearing Konrad's screams for longer than he had.

Although his initial feeling was relief at the silence around him, panic quickly took over when he realized what he had done. How the hell was he going to explain this? He then decided that he would not. He took the hockey stick and wiped it off with an old rag. He put the bloody rag in his pocket and decided to take the stick with him. Nobody would question a teenage boy carrying a hockey stick right before winter vacation. He was about to leave when he suddenly remembered the chalk dust on Konrad's face. He did not want to get too close, so he quickly filled a pail with water and splashed it mercilessly on the unconscious boy's face. Konrad made a sort of ugly choking sound but did not regain consciousness. Since the chalk dust was still fresh, most of it washed off immediately, leaving only a few unsightly white smears mixed with drying blood on Konrad's face. It was not perfect, but it would have to do. Yazin did not want to spend a minute longer in this place. He then remembered the keys. They were still in Konrad's pocket.

"Damn it!" he said aloud, but then decided that he would just leave the door open.

Even though the school was closing for the winter break, security personnel would still have to do their rounds. One of them would surely see the door open, find Konrad, and call an ambulance. Whatever happened after that, Yazin would have to worry about later. Right now, he just wanted to leave, and that is exactly what he did.

The ten days that followed were absolute torture for Yazin. He kept expecting the phone to ring with the news of Konrad's death, or his mother to come into his bedroom followed by two husky police officers that would drag him into a cell and lock him up for a long time. Although he was a minor, and the probability of this ever happening was incredibly slim, he had seen enough prison movies to know that the first thing inmates would to young boys is rape them as a welcome present. He would become the common bitch for inmates who felt they needed a woman but had to settle for the next best thing.

Yazin was not able to enjoy his winter break at all. He jumped every time the phone or doorbell rang. He stayed inside the entire time and became even more nervous when neither Leonardo nor Nelson returned his calls. He thought about calling Konrad's house, perhaps with the excuse of an unclear homework assignment, but decided against it. He was simply too scared. At night, he was haunted by nightmares of a one-legged Konrad hobbling after him with a mouthful of chalk bits and blood running from his eyes, nose, and ears. He would wake up from these drenched in sweat, and would turn on his bedside lamp, just to make sure Konrad was not in the room with him.

When it came time for school to begin again, Yazin had made a decision. If Konrad were alive and well, he would go over to him, and offer his most sincere apology, not only for what had happened the last time they had seen each other, but for all the years of pain and humiliation he had caused Konrad. He was genuinely sorry. If Konrad were willing, he would even try to be friends with him. After all, the two of them had been friends before, when they were in elementary school. It was a long shot, but why not? Stranger things had been known to happen. On the other hand, if Konrad were dead or seriously injured, he would go to the police, and confess everything. He would take his punishment like a man, and not even implicate Leonardo or Nelson. It was the least he could do.

The first day of the return to school came, and Konrad did not report to homeroom. Yazin stared at his empty desk nervously as he cracked his knuckles repeatedly. Perhaps he would see him during one of the later periods. The entire day went by, and Konrad did not show up for any of his classes. Yazin went home that afternoon with an uneasy mind. It was not uncommon for students to be absent the first few days after vacation. Sometimes families took a few extra days out of town with their children. The school's administration advised against it, but it was expected nonetheless.

That night, Yazin's nightmare was worse than ever. The half-rotting corpse of Konrad appeared at the foot of his bed. He was missing his left leg and was holding a hockey stick in his hands.

"You're going to get fucked, Hansur. You killed me, and now they're going to fuck you up the ass in prison. They're going to take one of these and thrust it so far up into you that it'll come out your mouth, and then you're going to wish you were the dead one."

Konrad then put the hockey stick on his crotch and made an obscene back-and-forth motion with it.

"That's right, Hansur. And then they're going to rip your balls off, and feed them to you," he continued with a demonic smile.

"I'm sorry, Forest," Yazin tried to say, but the words would not come out of his mouth.

He jerked out of his dream once again and bit his bedcovers to stifle the very real scream that was forming in his throat.

Two more weeks passed, and Konrad did not show up at school. This was definitely not normal. A couple of days was one thing, but two full weeks was quite another. On the last Friday of this fortnight, Yazin could no longer stand it. The last period of the day was homeroom, and he went to his teacher as the students were leaving.

"Ms. Lopez, is Konrad sick?"

The question seemed to make Lopez nervous. She was a pretty, young teacher fresh out of graduate school, and still in her twenties. She was popular with the students because of her youth, not to mention her good looks. However, also due to her age, she was a bit naïve, and did not always use her better judgement as Yazin found out that day.

"Are you a friend of his?" she asked in a conspiratorial tone. Yazin nodded. Lopez held her breath for a moment and waited for the last student to leave the classroom. When it was just the two of them, she answered.

"It's the strangest thing. When he didn't show up the first few days it seemed normal enough. I mean, parents sometimes take their kids on vacation and totally disregard school schedules."

Yazin waited patiently as Lopez voiced aloud the ideas that he himself had already considered.

"The thing is, when I called his house to find out what was wrong, there was no answer. I called his father's work number as well and they couldn't tell me anything."

"Anything about what?" Yazin asked.

"Anything about anything. The whole family just disappeared into thin air. Nobody has seen or heard from them in at least a week. Their house is empty. No one knows where they are."

Yazin had wanted an explanation for Konrad's absence, but he had never expected this. His teacher's answer did not set his mind at ease. Quite the contrary. What the hell was going on?

Yazin pondered this information repeatedly in his head, trying to make sense of it all. After a while, he started to calm down. Perhaps this was a blessing in disguise. Konrad's disappearance meant Yazin's problem would disappear too. If he stayed missing, there would be nothing to worry about.

About a week later, the news of the Forest family's disappearance became official. The school put up pictures of Konrad and his parents throughout Jackson Heights. The school principal even started a fund for the search efforts. The problem was that normally family members were the most interested in finding their loved ones. If an entire family went missing, who would continue looking for them? The answer was no one. By the time spring came around that year, everyone had lost interest in the Forest family. The flyers had come down, and the fund money was gaining interest in the principal's personal bank account.

On his part, Yazin had become a completely different

person. He cut ties completely with Leonardo, Nelson, and the other undesirable elements in his school and neighborhood. He studied hard and made good grades in his final quarter. His parents and teachers were pleasantly surprised, and at the commencement ceremony of Jackson Heights Junior High School that year, Yazin Hansur received the award for the student who had showed the most improvement. Yazin knew it was a bullshit award, but it made his parents proud, and that was something he was not used to, so he embraced it.

That summer his nightmares featuring Konrad became less and less frequent, and by the end of his vacation, he began wondering if he had perhaps just imagined the whole horrible ordeal to begin with.

He started high school and worked hard. He was never an exceptional student but made decent enough grades to keep his parents happy. In his senior year he turned eighteen, and had his name legally changed to Jason Hanson. He requested it appear that way on his diploma, much to the disappointment and bitterness of his father. After graduation, he moved into a rented room in Astoria and started severing the relationship with his parents. They were part of his old life and had nothing to do with his newly created Jason Hanson persona.

He worked for several years at various minimum wage jobs while going to college and was able to earn his degree in advertising by the time he was thirty. Starting his professional life at that age was a disadvantage, but he had a strong student portfolio, and was able to land his current job at *Empire Advertising*. He was now nearing his fifth anniversary at the company, and it was the first time in more than twenty years that he had thought about Konrad Forest, and what had happened that day at the After School Center.

Now, looking at this almost perfect mold of a man that was the adult version of Konrad Forest, Jason began to feel the stinging burn of jealousy creep into his heart. He thought about his own unattractive physique. He was not yet thirty-five, but already had a considerable belly, even though he was not fat. This made it even worse. At least, a fat man with a round belly looked proportional. Jason just looked like a lowercase letter b with feet. His annoyingly curly hair would not allow itself to be combed and was already quite thin on top. His eyebrows were so thick that they joined together between his eyes in a unibrow that his coworkers dubbed *Jason's Eye Moustache.* All of these were gross exaggerations of the truth, but in comparing himself to Konrad, it became very real in his mind. *The motherfucker must feel really good at seeing how the passage of time has treated us differently*, Jason thought bitterly.

"… Will show Forest the ropes, won't you Hanson?"

At the mention of his name, Jason snapped out of his daydream. "Pardon me, Mr. Thorpe. What was that?"

"I said that I'm putting Forest on your team, so he can learn how things are done here." Thorpe then turned to Konrad apologetically and said, "I know you have experience in Europe, kid, but we work a little differently in America, OK?"

"It is absolutely fine with me, sir," Konrad responded, and gave Jason another little smile.

Jason did not say a word. He simply nodded in acceptance and cracked his knuckles noisily without realizing he was doing it.

The never-ending meeting finally came to an end, and people started leaving the conference room. Jason walked over to Konrad, not without a touch of apprehension.

"Welcome to the team. Thorpe talks a lot, but he never actually introduced us properly. Jason Hanson." Jason put out his hand, not knowing what to expect.

Konrad shook his hand firmly. "Konrad Forest. It's a pleasure to meet you."

He doesn't remember me, Jason thought to himself. It made sense. Two decades had passed and he *did* have a different name now, but somehow, it did not feel quite right.

"Maybe we can…" Jason began.

"Konrad, would you like to have lunch with us?"

Both men turned around, and two, incredibly sexy women wearing miniskirts were looking their way. One was a brunette, and the other one a blonde. They had on business suits that were tight enough to cause men to stare at them, but not tight enough to be considered inappropriate work attire. The brunette was the one who had spoken.

"Oh… Thank you… I don't know…" Konrad turned to look at Jason.

"You can come too if you want to, Jason," the blonde said. Even though the words were technically an invitation, the tone was almost an insult. She may as well just have said *fuck you* to his face.

"That's all right, Konrad. You go ahead. I already have lunch plans," Jason said with a fake smile, and then turned to the women. "But thank you for the invitation. Perhaps on another occasion."

"Sure," the blonde said and took Konrad by the hand.

"I'll stop by your office first thing tomorrow morning. How does that sound?" Konrad asked as he was being led away by the two women.

"That sounds perfect. I'll see you then," Jason answered and muttered, "Sluts," under his breath.

"Did you say something, Jason?" the brunette asked.

"I said shucks, look at the time. I'm going to be late for my lunch date," Jason answered and walked away, but not before hearing the brunette tell the blonde that the only date Jason could ever get was either with a hooker or with an inflatable doll. This brought on giggles from both women. Once again, Konrad was the only one who did not laugh.

The following morning Konrad went over to Jason's office as agreed, and they went over the fundamentals. They discussed the mission and vision of the company and talked about Konrad's experience in Europe. Every now and then, Jason would ask Konrad a question about his past. He had to be sure that this was the same person he had known twenty years ago. Konrad had been born in Canada and grown up in Queens. He attended Jackson Heights Junior High School and moved to Europe as a teenager. He had moved back to the United States a year ago. The time frame of Konrad's move to Europe coincided with the mysterious disappearance of the Forest family, but Konrad did not offer any details, and Jason thought it unwise to insist too much. By the end of the day, Jason felt more at ease. Whatever may have happened long ago, Konrad was a healthy, successful professional, and, apart from the small, white scar above his eye, any other possible scars from his past seemed to have been completely erased.

Konrad was a talented artist, and a fast learner of the business. He became very well known in the company within a matter of months. He was the object of desire of many women he encountered, and quite a few of the men as well. The same women who had invited him to lunch on his first day had suggested a threesome a couple of weeks later. Konrad had politely declined what most other men would have pounced on in a heartbeat. He told them that if he ever got a divorce, they would be the first two people he would call. Of course, this only made them want him more. On top of everything else he had going for him, Konrad was happily married to a gorgeous Russian model with whom he shared a beautiful house in suburban Long Island.

Jason observed Konrad's career at Empire Advertising take off with growing resentment. He envied the charm and social graces which seemed to come so easily to Konrad. His family life also seemed to be caressed by a divine hand. About a year after Konrad had joined the company, his wife, Katrina, became pregnant. By the time he completed his second year at Empire Advertising, Konrad was the proud father of beautiful, healthy twin babies, a boy, and a girl.

It was indeed a difficult time for Jason. He looked at his own life – no children, no woman by his side, and apparently, not much possibility of either one in the foreseeable future. He would go on dates every now and then, and would spend the night with some of them, but it never blossomed into anything. To put it quite simply, he was miserable. Truth be told, life had not changed much for Jason since Konrad had reentered his life, but seeing the contrast made him even *more* aware of his unhappy existence. During this time, Jason's jealousy of Konrad had grown steadily, but he could not quite bring himself to hate the man. After all, he had never done anything to him. Quite the contrary. Any time Konrad was praised on a job well done, he would make sure that Jason was acknowledged as his mentor. He would thank Jason constantly for his help, which, at times, would even become annoying. He had even invited Jason to his home on a couple of occasions for dinner. Not that this did much to soothe Jason. Seeing Konrad's happy home, equipped with dazzling wife and adorable, bouncing babies made Jason's blood boil.

The years passed, and as the men approached forty, Jason let himself go completely. He gained about fifty pounds, which put him close to the two-hundred eighty mark. By now, he was completely bald on top and his remaining rebellious hair on the sides made him look like 'Krusty The Clown' from 'The Simpsons.' In sharp contrast, Konrad had begun to show some attractive gray on the sides and grown a beard. He looked less like a pretty boy, and more like a mature, family man, but he still caused women to sigh dreamily when they saw him, perhaps even more so than before.

Jason's career was going pretty much the same as when he had first started in the company. Just as he had never been an exceptional student, he was not an exceptional professional either. His ideas were fine, and the campaigns were successful enough to sell products and make the company money. However, it was nothing to all the pomp and circumstance Konrad would receive, especially by Thorpe, who had pretty much adopted Konrad as his golden boy. Thorpe had not gotten any more dignified with age, and would slap Konrad on the back, or pinch his cheeks as a sign of affection. Konrad took it all with quiet resignation and amusement.

Seeing that his professional life had become stagnant, Jason started paying a young man from his neighborhood to develop campaigns for him. Moe was a scruffy young artist with a serious cocaine addiction. He would produce his best work while under the influence, and charge Jason next to nothing for his services. Jason knew that all the money he gave Moe went straight up his nose because he was always broke, but that was not his problem.

Moe was a big boy and responsible for his own actions. Another interesting fact about Moe was the meeting points he would dream up. He was obviously into the whole cloak-and-dagger experience, but Jason played along. It was a small price to pay for the junkie's work.

One time, the meeting place designated by Moe was Fresh Kills, the garbage landfill on Staten Island. Jason had to take a subway to the ferry, a ferry to the island, and a cab to the landfill. This was becoming extreme, and more than a bit ridiculous. Jason would have to have a serious talk with Moe. There had to be a more convenient arrangement than this.

When Jason arrived, Moe was pacing back and forth like a father-to-be in the maternity ward.

"What took you so long, man?" Moe asked reproachfully.

"I'm five minutes early," Jason responded looking at his watch. "Do you have it?"

Moe looked around uneasily. "Yeah… It's kind of like… I mean I do, and I don't, you know?"

Jason began to feel the vein in his right temple throb. Moe's constant movement was irritating him, but he kept his composure.

"No, I don't know. What does that mean?"

Moe took out a crumpled piece of paper from inside his jacket and handed it to Jason. Jason unfolded it, and there were a few rough sketches done in pencil.

"What the fuck is this?" Jason asked angrily.

"It's a rough draft, man. You know, the main idea."

Jason grabbed Moe roughly but the collar of his jacket.

"I'm not paying you for a main idea, asshole. I need the complete copy and storyboards. That is our arrangement."

Moe just dangled limply from Jason's grip.

"I know, dude. I... I... Just give me some more time, OK?"

Jason let go and Moe crumpled to the ground.

"It's Thursday evening. My presentation is on Monday morning. When do you suppose you'll have it done?"

Moe stayed on the ground. He looked up at Jason pleadingly.

"I'm fast, man. You know that. I'm just out of blow. That's all. Maybe if I could have an advance for next time..."

Jason prepared himself to kick Moe, but the young man put his arms up defensively and started crying.

"I need my candy, dude. I can't deliver without my stuff. Come on, man. Help a brother out." He sobbed.

Jason looked at his disgusting display of human decadence. He had no idea why Moe had referred to himself as a brother. He was not black, and he certainly did not seem to belong to any religious order as far as Jason could tell. Who knew what went on in these lowlifes' heads? However, Jason's continued employment at Empire Advertising depended on this particular lowlife at the moment, and the presentation deadline was too close to come up with a new plan by now.

Jason took out five twenty-dollar bills, and threw them at Moe, who scooped them up like an eager child collecting candy after breaking a pinata.

"It'll be good, dude. Better than anything I've ever done for you before. It'll be brilliant!" Moe squealed.

"It had better be," Jason said, and left Moe sitting on the ground in front of the landfill, caressing his newly acquired treasure and fantasizing about the amazing sensations it would buy him.

Jason was extremely annoyed, and more than a bit nervous as well. Tonight, Moe would probably snort himself unconscious, which left only Friday and Saturday to come up with an impressive campaign, so that Jason could study it and memorize it on Sunday. It was cutting it close, but he decided he did not have a choice, and temporarily put the situation out of his mind. It is important to point out that Jason obviously *did* have a choice, which was to work hard, and come up with the campaign himself over the weekend. After all, that was his job. Sadly, the thought never even crossed his mind.

That Saturday, Konrad invited Jason over to his house for lunch. He had recently acquired a jacuzzi, and Konrad suggested they could both use some rest and relaxation before their big presentations on Monday. Jason accepted the invitation. He knew he would be sick with envy, but the idea of soaking in a jacuzzi during this stressful time was just too tempting.

After lunch and some meaningless conversation, Konrad and Jason began changing into their bathing suits. Katrina had taken the babies upstairs for a bath, and then said she would take a nap with them. Jason observed her intently. She was dressed simply in lounge pants and a t-shirt but was still the most exotically beautiful woman he had ever seen in his life. He could hardly believe that there had once been two human beings growing inside such a perfect body. He felt the monster of jealousy stirring inside him, but quickly squashed it with an idea. He would picture Katrina in his mind the next time he had sex. Why hadn't he thought of that before?

As they were changing, Jason's eye caught something that he did not identify at first. Right above Konrad's left knee, there was a series of small straps connected to small metallic circles that went completely around his leg. When he looked more closely, he realized what it was. Konrad had a prosthetic. This charming Adonis of a man was walking around with a fake leg.

Feeling Jason's brazen stare, Konrad spoke.

"Most people don't know. That's German engineering for you," he said tapping the rubberized plastic. "I'm not trying to hide it, but I don't advertise it either, you understand."

"What happened?" Jason asked, genuinely surprised at what he had discovered.

"I lost my leg when I was a teenager. It was a long time ago. Gangrene."

A sickening rush of memories came flooding back to Jason. He could see a thirteen-year-old Konrad dangling upside down and crying hysterically. Scenes of the many nightmares he had experienced twenty-five years ago filled his mind. His throat seemed to close, and his tongue felt like sandpaper, but he managed to speak.

"I'm sorry," he said.

Jason was apologizing for what he had done when they were teenagers, but in this context, it was pretty much what any person would have said, not a truly heartfelt apology to the common ear.

"Yes," Konrad continued. "The problem was the injury wasn't treated in time. If I had been found sooner, the doctors could have saved my leg, but I was unconscious for quite a long time before receiving any medical attention.

Jason felt sick to his stomach, but he needed to pull himself together. Konrad did not remember him. What had happened had happened a long time ago, and there was nothing he could do to make it better. He forced himself to ask.

"What kind of injury did you suffer?"

"Hockey," Konrad replied, smiling a little. "It can be such a violent sport."

On his train ride home that night, Jason was an emotional mess. Overdue feelings of guilt took hold of his heart and mind and made him very uneasy. By the time he reached the Woodside station of the Long Island Railroad, he was crying. From there, it was only a short subway ride to Astoria, but it gave him enough time to make a decision. The plan was quite simple in its complexity. Tomorrow he would pick up the package from Moe, and no longer have anything to do with the junkie. On Monday morning, he would impress everyone with his presentation in the morning and take the afternoon off. He would take Konrad to lunch and reveal who he was, and what their relationship had been in the past. He would confess everything, and he would do something that he should have done a long time ago. He would apologize. It would be a sincere, sentimental apology, twenty-five years in the making.

He did not expect Konrad to forgive him. He would probably not grant forgiveness if the tables had been turned, but he needed to go through with it, nonetheless. In the end, Konrad's reaction would not really change anything. Jason's plan was to never see him again after that. On Tuesday morning, Thorpe would receive an e-mail from Jason informing him that he could shove his job up his fat ass and confessing that the campaigns presented in the last few years by Jason had been the work of a strung-out loser who could barely function unless he received a constant stream of nose candy. It was not a very honorable way to leave a company, but in Jason's twisted estimation, the shame would serve as a sort of purgatory for him.

Early Sunday morning, Jason got a call from Moe. As usual, his meeting place of choice was a shady, abandoned tenement building in the Flatbush area of Brooklyn. He would be waiting inside apartment 3H at noon. Annoyed by the inconvenient arrangement, Jason confirmed the meeting. It would be the last time, anyway.

When he arrived at the building, he discovered that not only was it condemned, but it was scheduled to be demolished the following day, first thing in the morning. There was a rusty, barbwire fence surrounding the premises, and several signs that read: HAZARDOUS AREA. DO NOT ENTER. TRESPASSERS WILL BE SUBJECT TO ARREST. Jason grunted. How the hell was he supposed to get in? He looked around and saw only one option. The fence did not appear to be electrified. He would have to climb it. This was not going to be an easy task for Jason, who was carrying around a lot of extra weight these days. He would probably cut his hands and get an infection when he crossed over, provided he could even make it to the top at all. He could very well have a heart attack on the way up. And how would he get back out? He would have to do it all over again.

"Son of a bitch," Jason said aloud.

Luckily for Jason, the fence was not too tall, but it took him almost twenty minutes to complete the feat anyway. As he had expected, he tore the skin of both hands going over and scratched his stomach pretty badly as well. He came crashing down on both feet on the other side, and felt his kidneys protest in agony. He got himself together, wiping sweat and blood off his clothes and person as well as he could. He then froze as he looked through the fence. He had left his bag on the other side. Jason looked at his watch. It was already past twelve-thirty. He would have to risk leaving his bag behind, and hope it was still there when he came back. The coke head might get desperate and leave.

Jason hurried along the dirty path that led to the building and entered it. The place was an absolute dump. The walls were almost completely peeled, displaying countless coats of cheap paint. There were nests of rats everywhere, and they scurried brazenly over Jason's feet as he walked into the building. He stepped on a couple, and kicked others away, for which he received a strident chorus of angry squeals. He was afraid that the rats might organize themselves and attack him, so he made his way up the crumbling stairs quickly to the third floor. It was perhaps a bit too quickly because he arrived completely out of breath, and with a sharp pain in his chest. When he could breathe again, he made his way down a dark and dirty corridor to apartment 3H. The door was slightly ajar, so he let himself in, and asked in a wheezy voice, "Moe?"

The apartment seemed empty. It was supported by a couple of cement columns in what Jason supposed was the living room. He walked in a little further, and suddenly felt a blunt, hot pain in the back of his head. The world went black, and he lost consciousness.

Yazin and his friends, Leonardo and Nelson, stood next to the punch bowl in the gymnasium of Jackson Heights Junior High School. It had been very nicely decorated by a committee of eighth graders, but it was obviously still a gymnasium. The basketball hoops and the hockey posts were a dead giveaway. It was the first dance of the school year, and the theme was *Welcome to Junior High,* so it was the first dance ever for most of the attendees. Yazin nudged his friends as Konrad entered the gymnasium. He was dressed in a dark, gray, three-piece suit, and he looked stiff and uncomfortable. His hair had been neatly parted on the left side and was slicked down with his father's Vitalis.

Konrad felt embarrassment almost instantly when he walked through the door. Most of the kids were wearing jeans and sneakers. The girls may have had a little extra make-up, and the boys a little extra gel, but that was basically it. He had told his mother that kids no longer dressed this way for dances, but she had insisted that no son of hers would attend a social event looking like a bum. He had consented but put his foot down when his mother suggested he go with his older sister. This he would not do, and, luckily for him, his father had sided with him, and convinced his mother that it was best that Konrad go alone. Konrad looked around nervously, and briefly considered leaving, but instead walked to the punch bowl without realizing he was walking straight into the wolves' den.

Yazin did not waste any time. "Hey, Forest. Where's the stockbroker's convention?"

"Huh?" Konrad said distractedly, and then took an unconscious step backward when he saw who his company was.

"The threads, man. What's with the suit?" Leonardo and Nelson just snickered next to Yazin like mindless henchmen.

Konrad turned around and was about to walk away when Yazin grabbed him by the arm in a friendly manner.

"Relax, Forest. I'm just playing with you. It's actually a good thing that you wore the suit tonight."

Konrad just looked at him, uncomprehending.

"I'm serious, man. I hear Jenny has the hots for you."

Konrad shook Yazin's arm off and simply said, "Leave me alone."

Leonardo and Nelson took this as a sign of aggression, and were about to interfere, but Yazin held them back.

"There's no problem here, guys," he said. "I'm just letting Forest know that he has a not-so-secret admirer. It's his problem if he chooses to ignore it. If a chick as hot as Jenny were into me…"

Konrad did not hear the rest because he had already walked

away, but Yazin's words had made an impression on him. The Jenny in question was Jennifer Richardson. She was not only the hottest girl in the eighth grade, but also the most popular. She was the perfect example of the All-American dream girl: blonde, blue eyes, great smile, and a toned, athletic body. Konrad had fantasized about her on many occasions but had not even come close to trying to talk to her. It would never work. He was a seventh grader, and the word was that she only dated high school guys. Most of the boys at Jackson Heights Junior High School had a crush on her, Konrad included. Could it be that what Yazin was saying was true? No, that was impossible. Or was it?

"Hi, Konrad."

Konrad jumped at the sound of the voice behind him. As if he had summoned her with his thoughts, Jenny was standing there in her full splendor. She was wearing a denim mini-skirt and high-top, Converse sneakers. She had her hair in a high ponytail and looked like a cheerleader in a teen movie.

"Hi," Konrad managed to respond after a few moments. He could not believe this goddess was talking to him.

"Do you want to dance?" she asked with a coquettish smile.

Konrad looked around as if to make sure the question was directed toward him, and looked back at Jenny, not completely understanding.

"Yes. I'm talking to you, silly. Come on."

She took him by the hand and led him to the dance floor. Konrad followed awkwardly, hypnotized by Jenny's beauty. The DJ started playing 'Careless Whisper' by George Michael, and Konrad almost fainted. There was no way he could pull off a slow song with Jenny. It was too much pressure. They started dancing, and Jenny pulled him close to her. Konrad felt the beginning of an erection, and tried to back away, but Jenny only pushed up more against him. The feeling of her breasts on his chest made him stiffen immediately, in every sense of the word. Jenny simply smiled and whispered in his ear.

"It's OK. I'm into you too."

Konrad could not believe his good fortune. George Michael continued wailing about how he was never going to dance again due to the lack of rhythm in his guilty feet when Jenny gave Konrad what was unmistakably a look of sexual desire and said, "Let's get out of here."

Konrad followed her off the dance floor, and they went into the boys' locker room. The adult chaperones at the dance were too busy having a good time and hitting on each other to even Notice Jenny and Konrad slip out of the gymnasium.

As soon as they were alone, Jenny pushed him against a set of lockers roughly, and started kissing him voraciously. Konrad had never kissed a girl in his life. He had dreamt about it many times, but he had never imagined that the sensation would be so intense throughout his entire body. Jenny moaned sensually as she allowed him to caress her awkwardly and inexpertly. She said, "Tell me you want me."

"I want you," Konrad said obediently.

"Louder," she said raising her voice.

"I want you," Konrad repeated, adding some volume.

Jenny undid his pants and pulled down his underwear. When she grabbed hold of his penis, he thought he would explode.

"I can't hear you," she said aggressively.

"I want you! I want you! I want you!" Konrad almost screamed.

Jenny let go and took several steps back.

"Well, you can't have me," she said and then yelled out, "do it now!"

Yazin, Leonardo and Nelson jumped out from behind another set of lockers. Yazin had a Polaroid camera in his hands and took a picture of Konrad in his lamentable state. The other boys and Jenny howled with laughter. It took Konrad a few moments to understand what was happening, and then his face contorted in terror. He looked at Yazin, who now had the developed picture in his hand, and said in a slow and serious voice, "Please, Yazin. Don't do it."

Their eyes locked together for a moment, and Yazin faltered just the slightest bit. He could read the panic in Konrad's eyes, and understood what he was thinking. To be honest, Yazin had never had the intention of making the photo public. He just wanted to play a nasty joke on the nerd, and show it to his inner circle of hoodlums, so they could have a good laugh about it later. But Yazin saw clearly in Konrad's eyes that he was terrified it would be seen by the entire school.

"I'm not going to…" Yazin began, but Leonardo had already snatched the picture out of his hand and was showing it to Nelson and Jenny.

Seeing this, Konrad pulled up his pants, and charged Leonardo with the force of a linebacker, causing the two of them to fall to the floor. The photo flew out of Leonardo's hand, and Nelson picked it up, handing it over to Jenny for safe keeping. Nelson then tried to pull Konrad off Leonardo but was suddenly surprised when Konrad elbowed him hard in the ribs, causing him to gasp. Yazin was speechless. This was the first time he had seen Konrad fight back, and he was doing a damn good job at it. At that moment, Yazin felt a combination of pity and admiration for Konrad, but such noble feelings lasted only a few seconds.

He went over to where the brawl was taking place and got Konrad into a full nelson. Leonardo and Nelson saw the opportunity and started punching Konrad steadily in the chest and stomach. Konrad started gasping, and Yazin let him fall to the floor where Leonardo and Nelson continued the beating by kicking Konrad in the ribs. All the while Jenny just stood in the corner, looking as helpless and innocent as can be. An outsider would have thought that she was the victim instead of one of the aggressors.

When he thought Konrad had had enough, Yazin told the other boys to back off. He crouched down to where Konrad was still gasping and said, "Jenny is going to hold on to the photo. If you tell absolutely anyone what went on here tonight, I will make sure the entire school gets a copy. Do you understand?"

Konrad remained silent, but Yazin knew his silence meant resignation. It was a lose-lose situation for Konrad, and, like all the other previous times, he would simply keep quiet about it. People like Konrad were not tattletales. They would suffer in silence, hoping that divine justice would compensate them in the future. Fat chance! There was never any danger of Konrad's photo becoming public. Jenny threw it away that very night. She didn't want her parents to come across a naked twelve-year-old boy in her dresser. Nelson's older brother, who was Jenny's official boyfriend, would not be too thrilled either. He had been the connection to Jenny, but he did not know the nature of the prank. He only knew that his girlfriend was going to help his kid brother and his friends play a joke on some loser in their school, and was perfectly comfortable with that.

The memory of the dance started fading in Jason's mind as he came to. He saw a mature, extremely good-looking Konrad staring at him. He tried to move but felt a sharp, jabbing pain all around his body, not to mention the dull pain in the back of his head. He had been tied to one of the cement columns with rope, but that was not the cause of his pain. He had also been wrapped in a sort of blanket made of rusty barbwire. Any small movement he made caused his skin to be pierced by the wire, so he had to remain as still as a statue if he did not want to become a heap of tattered flesh.

When Konrad was sure Jason was fully awake, he spoke.

"Welcome back, Yazin. This is the part where I go into a lengthy monologue explaining my detailed plot for revenge, but I'm going to spare you the bullshit. We both know what we know, and that is about the thick and thin of it. Goodbye."

As he saw Konrad walking away, Jason wanted to say many things. It could not just end like this. Where was the dramatic dialogue? Where was the final confrontation between enemies that had once been friends? The very least Konrad could do is go through the lengthy dialogue detailing his perfect crime. Isn't that how it always happened in the movies? Jason wanted to tell Konrad that he had felt remorse for his actions. True, it had taken a quarter of a century, but it was still valid, wasn't it? What was the statute of limitations on apologies anyway? It could simply not finish so insipidly. Jason needed a gut-wrenching, emotional finale to begin his previously planned, self-imposed journey into purgatory. Jason wanted desperately to explain all of this to Konrad, but the words that came out of his mouth sounded as empty as the apartment he was sitting in.

"I was going to apologize," he said meekly.

Konrad turned around with fire in his eyes, but his voice remained calm.

"You were *going* to apologize? When was this *going* to happen, or did you need another twenty-five years to think about it?"

Jason could not think of anything to say. He watched

helplessly as Konrad exited the apartment, the building, and his life. He suddenly remembered the scheduled demolition, and tried to move, but was quickly and painfully reminded of his dire situation. He started to cry, and his chest started heaving rapidly. He closed his eyes and traveled back in his mind to his first meeting with Konrad at Jackson Heights Elementary School.

Yazin was playing by himself with a Skeletor action figure in a corner of the playground. Skeletor was his favorite character in the Masters of the Universe cartoon that he watched on television after school, even though he was a villain. A couple of boys had approached him. They were the toughest boys in the school, and they were always together. He did not remember the details of the exchange, but the outcome had been that the boys had hit him and taken his action figure. Yazin had cried bitterly. This was his only expensive toy, and his mother would be incredibly angry with him because she had had to tighten her belt even more than usual to buy it for him.

From a short distance, Konrad had observed what had happened, but decided to wait a few minutes before walking over. Yazin was still crying when Konrad spoke to him.

"Hi. Do you want to play Masters of the Universe?"

Still sniffling, Yazin looked up. "Those guys took my Skeletor," he grumbled.

"Leonardo and Nelson are just a couple of bullies. Don't let them get to you."

Konrad had a He-Man action figure in his right hand. This was the hero of Masters of the Universe, Skeletor's archenemy. In his left hand, he had a Skeletor action figure. Yazin just stared at him.

"I'll be He-Man, and you can be Skeletor," Konrad continued.

"OK," Yazin finally said and stopped crying.

The two boys sat together and played for the remainder of the recess period. When it was time to line up for class, Yazin handed the Skeletor action figure back to Konrad. Konrad seemed to consider something for a moment, and then said, "You keep him. That way each of us has one, and when we're alone, we can still play Masters of the Universe."

Yazin could not believe that this boy was giving up such a precious toy to a stranger. It was the nicest thing anyone had ever done for him. He was deeply touched, and perhaps that was the reason why he said what he did.

"My name is Yazin. Do you want to be my best friend?"

Now it was Konrad's turn to be touched.

"I'm Konrad. Sure. I'll be your best friend."

The boys gave each other a high five, a childhood solidification of their newfound friendship.

Reflections

Felix was sweating bullets. His dress shirt stuck to his body like an extra layer of skin, but he did not dare take off his blazer, as it would expose a gray shirt that was completely soaked through, with especially sinister patches accumulating in the armpit regions. In the morning rush he had also forgotten his handkerchief, which was used to dry the sweat from his face, neck and head on a regular basis. Felix's case was extreme. For him, perspiration did not depend on weather. It could be the dead of winter, which it happened to be on this day, *Valentine's Day* to be exact, and Felix would be drenched from head to toe. He had even consulted several medical specialists about the situation. He tried beverages, powders, and pills to no avail. The last doctor he saw even suggested a surgery that would involve removing a nerve from the back of his neck that controlled the sweat glands. Problem or not, this solution was beyond what Felix was willing to try, so he just resigned himself to his sweaty existence.

It was especially bad when he was nervous, and today was his first day as Training Specialist at Professional Document Services in Times Square. Please don't let her be hot! Please don't let her be hot! Felix implored to no one in particular, as he was a confirmed atheist. The existence or lack of hotness of the *her* in question would be determined in the next fifteen minutes or so. Felix was expecting his first trainee, and he knew that she was a twenty-two-year-old who had recently graduated from

Riverdale University with a degree in business. She had been hired as a Quality Control Specialist and was to be under Felix's supervision for the next three months.

Now, granted, Quality Control Specialist at Professional Document Services sounds impressive and looks quite nice on a business card, but Felix knew first-hand it was a joke. Professional Document Services was a company that made photocopies, not much more than a glorified Kinko's with the clarification that Kinko's provided far superior services in a much more pleasant environment. It was housed on the tenth floor of a building that looked like it should be condemned. In fact, the only other floors occupied in the twelve-story structure, were the second floor, which was a company that made face creams, and the sixth floor where Sweet Cherry Productions made films. Felix wondered about the sanitary conditions surrounding the cream business, but the fact that insanely attractive people were always seen in bathrobes when the elevator door opened on the sixth floor left little to the imagination regarding the genre of the films that were being produced.

Felix had also been hired as a Quality Control Specialist right out of college five years ago. The hierarchy was as follows: the people who ran the copy machines were called Document Specialists and earned ten dollars an hour. The Quality Control Specialist made sure that the copies were made properly, bumping them up to twelve dollars an hour. Finally, the Training Specialists would act as supervisor of new employees and made a whopping fifteen dollars an hour. So, after five years in the bustling center of Times Square, crossroads of New York City and the world, Felix was making the same that a high school dropout in Seattle would make flipping burgers. Although a bit embarrassed by these circumstances, Felix was not particularly bitter about them. He had his eye on a sales position. That was where the real money was. Rinky-dink operation though it was, Professional Document Services were geniuses at marketing, and their top salespeople easily cleared six figures a year without counting bonuses. Of course, you would rarely see these luminaries at the Times Square building, and when they did make an appearance, the worker bees might as well be roaches by the looks they received from the visitors – a combination of pity and disgust that was rarely, if ever, disguised.

Notwithstanding the occasional humiliation, Felix figured that a couple of years as a Training Specialist would give him a strong lead-in to a sales position, and by the time his ten-year anniversary at the company came along, he would no longer be on the receiving end of the degrading looks.

The arrival of the new trainee abruptly pulled Felix out of his daydream, and he was unable to suppress the "Shit!" that came out of his mouth in time.

The young woman in front of him seemed more amused than offended and simply said, "Not really the welcome I was expecting. Are you Mr. Dupont?"

Embarrassed at his lack of decorum, Felix stood up quickly and offered his hand. "Sorry," he stammered, "I wasn't expecting you until nine o'clock. Felix Dupont."

"Britney Chase. I figured I'd come in early on my first day. You know, make a good impression."

She said this with a pleasant smile that, instead of putting Felix at ease, made him more nervous. He realized he had held on to her hand longer than normal and cursed internally when he heard the squelching sound his sweaty hand made when he released hers. Britney's face did not show a single trace of discomfort although it could not have possibly been an agreeable experience for her. Why did he always get so nervous around pretty girls?

After the preliminary awkwardness was over, Felix breathed a sigh of relief when the office manager, Mr. Davis, offered to give Britney a personal tour of the place. He knew that Davis saw her as a future sexual conquest, as he did with all new attractive female employees. It afforded Felix the opportunity to rush into the restroom and clean himself up, and that was presently more important than concerning himself with chivalry and protecting Britney's honor. The restrooms on the tenth floor were out of order and the nearest functioning ones were two floors down. Felix bounded down the stairway and burst into the eighth-floor men's room like a maniac.

The place was repulsive. It stank of everything you could possibly imagine and then some. The grimy walls looked like something out of a Saw film, there were rusted pipes everywhere and the mirrors barely provided a reflection because they were either cracked, scratched, or covered with graffiti. Felix pulled off his blazer and draped it over a sink that had probably not been scrubbed in the past decade. If Felix had stood under a shower, he would have been drier. His shirt was completely soaked through, and even his pants were beginning to feel humid. This was not normal. He removed his shirt and wrung it out desperately as sweat spilled out of it onto the cracked tile flooring. He felt like there were open faucets in his hair and behind his ears gushing out copious quantities of warm, salty liquid down his back and chest.

"Why did she have to be so hot?" he nearly screamed aloud, immediately covering his mouth, realizing how psychotic he must sound. He unbuckled his pants and let them drop to the floor, remaining only in his briefs, socks, and shoes. By this time, unnaturally large puddles of sweat had begun forming all around him and his shoes and socks were soon drenched as well. He tore off his remaining clothes and thought wildly, *What the hell is going on?* as he stood stark naked in the middle of a public men's room.

Felix tried to get a hold of himself, but everything around him was the stuff of nightmares. The room was now flooding, and the sea of sweat had reached Felix's knees. The rusty faucets started gushing warm liquid, and even though Felix did not touch it, he knew it was sweat as well. Suddenly, Felix saw his reflection in one of the cracked mirrors and started slogging through the sludgy liquid to get a better look. By the time he reached it, the restroom had filled to waist level with sweat. Felix had never felt so hot and uncomfortable in his life. The insanity of what was happening around him paled in comparison to the level of physical discomfort that he was feeling, so much so that he felt he would be willing to sell his soul for some relief and articulated the words aloud while staring at his fragmented reflection in the mirror. Although not a bad-looking young man, Felix was extremely thin, and that was the first thing that people noticed about him, whether they commented on it or not. As he was also over six feet tall, he appeared even taller due to his frame, and, being self-conscious about his body, had the tendency to slouch as well.

Felix leaned in toward the mirror until his nose was just a few inches away from the glass. Suddenly, his reflection's lips curled into a snarl and said, "Your word is your bond."

The terror that Felix felt was so great that he fell backwards into the pool of sweat that had filled the restroom. He was completely enveloped in the nasty substance and felt himself drowning. He flailed and kicked in a futile attempt to escape, but as he tried to scream, his mouth filled with the toxic sludge from his own body, and as he felt that his time on earth was coming to an end, he closed his eyes in resignation.

"I do the same thing, you know," a pleasant, young male voice made Felix open his eyes again.

He was standing in front of the dirty mirror, completely naked, and whipped around nervously at the sound of the words. In front of him was a muscular, attractive young man with long, golden hair that fell around his shoulders, dressed only in a white bathrobe and flip flops. There was a logo of a red cherry on his lapel. As if suddenly realizing his nakedness, Felix made a motion to cover up, but realized his clothes was strewn all about the restroom. The young man chuckled and said, "Is this your first shoot? Don't worry. You'll get used to it."

Felix's confused mind could not make heads or tails of these words, so all he could manage was a weak, *"What?"*

"I get it. You're in character. You're playing the geeky IT guy who services the bored housewife's laptop, right? I'll leave you to it, but practicing in front of the mirror, classic method, dude. Good for you."

It took a moment for Felix to grasp what was happening, but since it was probably easier to pretend to be an amateur porn actor for thirty seconds instead of having to explain why he had stripped in a public restroom, he went with it.

"Thanks," he replied.

The young actor winked at him and was gone. Felix dressed quickly and rushed back upstairs to his office. Mr. Davis approached him, followed by Britney.

"Felix will take care of you now. Welcome aboard," he said to Britney with a forced smile. Felix looked at his watch and then at Mr. Davis questioningly. Barely five minutes had elapsed since Felix had left the office.

"You're already done?"

"Yeah," answered Mr. Davis loudly. And then he leaned in close to Felix and added in a whisper, "Not worth it. Bitch won't put out. Have fun!" He slapped Felix roughly on the back and walked away.

Felix looked at Britney, and she gave him a warm smile. She reminded him a little of Laura Vandervoort. She had the type of beauty that can be attributed to a wholesome girl-next-door type just as easily as it could be to an exotic dancer, and this was a combination that made Felix even more uncomfortable than he usually was in the presence of attractive women. Out of habit, he reached for his handkerchief, remembered that he had left it at home, and then cursed at himself internally. He would have to wipe his brow with his hands. As he did so he was completely unprepared for what he felt, or rather for what he did not feel. There was not a drop of sweat on his forehead, or anywhere else for that matter. Felix was completely dry.

To say that the first day of training with Britney went smoothly for Felix would be misleading. Dry or not, he was still socially awkward, and very self-conscious about his body. However, the fact that he was not sweating at all was something less to worry about, and he got through the day. Britney was very polite and attentive, took notes and asked questions. She smiled frequently, and laughed at Felix's attempts at jokes whether they were funny or not. In short, despite his nervousness, Felix enjoyed playing mentor to such an agreeable person, and when he got home that night, he was feeling happy.

Of course, as with many other pleasant emotions, his happiness was short-lived when he realized that Britney was dominating his thoughts. This had happened to Felix many times in the past. He would meet a pretty girl that was nice to him, misinterpret her behavior as potential romantic interest, and be sorely disappointed when he realized it was not. It is important to note that this entire process mostly took place in Felix's mind. He rarely, if ever, took any steps to explore the possibility of romance with them, and simply anticipated rejection as the inevitable outcome before even trying anything. He almost preferred the nasty ones who knew they were too hot for him, and either ignored him completely, or had sex with him and then ignored him after the fact. At least with these types there were no castles in the sky. Deciding to be practical, Felix filed Britney away as one more unattainable relationship and settled in to watch reruns of 'The Twilight Zone' on television.

He heard the familiar crackling sounds of the radiator in the studio apartment where he lived in Hell's Kitchen and settled in for another uncomfortable, sleepless night. It was the middle of February, so Felix could certainly appreciate the need for heating, but the building where he lived was mostly occupied by elderly people who constantly complained of the cold, so the landlord would regularly keep the thermostat at seventy-five degrees, sometimes even cranking it up to eighty degrees if the tenants requested it, to avoid any legal issues. Felix suffered through it because he had a sweet deal with a rent-controlled apartment that had originally been occupied by his grandparents in the 1940s. Seventy-five years later he was paying $500 a month for the place which was unheard of in New York, especially in such a central location.

In preparation, Felix took out several t-shirts. On especially cold nights, the heat would be more like a sauna, and he would have to change several times during the night and still wake up in a puddle of his own sweat. The incessant commercials referencing Valentine's Day did not help his mood either. It was going to be a long night.

The following morning, Felix woke up feeling refreshed after a night of uninterrupted sleep. He walked into the bathroom and started undressing. He would always turn his clothes inside out and hang them on the towel rack to dry before placing them in the laundry hamper, but he suddenly realized that he was wearing the same t-shirt that he had gone to bed in – it was completely dry. Surprised, Felix looked at the thermostat – eighty-eight degrees – impossible. He should be drenched by now. He peered out the door, and saw the pile of dry t-shirts, still folded, sitting unused on a chair. He suddenly remembered what had happened the day before and thought, *The mirror.* That has to be it. Not quite convinced about his own conclusion, he stared hard at himself for a good five minutes in the bathroom mirror, waiting for something to happen. When nothing did, feeling more than a bit foolish, he sighed and stepped into the shower.

At work, he continued his training of Britney, and even though he had resolved just the night before to write her off as a *never going to happen*, he could not help being fascinated by her flawless skin, sweet smile, and the way she would toss her hair back when it fell over her face. Felix caught himself staring longingly at her on more than one occasion and had to check himself. He did not know if Britney caught sight of it too, but if she did, she showed no sign of it. At least he was not sweating.

A couple of hours into the workday, Felix started feeling an itching sensation on his head. He occasionally suffered from dry scalp, especially during the winter, but it was under control due to a medicated shampoo that he used during the cold months. This time it seemed to be more persistent than usual, so he scratched his head, releasing a small flurry of white flakes that settled on his shoulders. Luckily, Britney was not facing him now, so he was able to shake them off discreetly. As the day progressed, the itching sensation got stronger, and spread to his sideburns and cheeks. Every time he scratched at them minute particles of dead skin floated down onto his clothing. By the time the workday was over, the sensation had taken over his whole body, and no matter how much he scratched, he could not find relief. He left abruptly without saying goodbye to anyone and raced down to the eighth-floor restroom once again. The room was in as deplorable state as ever, but he noticed that although the cracks and scratches were still there, the mirror did not have any trace of graffiti on it.

Felix peered apprehensively into the mirror and saw that entire scabs of dead skin had formed on his eyebrows and nose. As he picked at them, they fell into nasty clumps into the sink in front of him and started reforming before his very eyes. The more he tried to peel them off his face, the faster they would form. The itching in his scalp became unbearable, and he was now scratching violently, digging his nails deep into the flesh and drawing blood. "What the fuck? Stop it already!" he screamed at no one in particular, but his words caught the attention of the reflection in the mirror as they had the day before. Felix's reflection stared at him in vexation.

"Really, my friend. You are a most difficult man to please."

At any other moment, Felix would have been scared out of his wits, but considering the events of the last couple of days, he was willing to engage in conversation with his reflection.

"Make it stop," he ordered harshly.

"As you wish," answered the reflection, and Felix was back to his normal self, staring at his reflection with a layer of perspiration already forming on his face.

"What is this?" Felix asked in a slightly calmer tone, although he felt anything but.

The reflection stared back and gave a heavy sigh of resignation as someone who is preparing to explain an amazingly simple concept to a very slow person.

"You were unhappy with your current circumstances, so I provided you with an alternative."

"Right," snapped Felix. "You thought that an adequate solution for excessive perspiration was extreme dehydration?"

The reflection looked like a naughty child who had been scolded after playing a particularly nasty prank, but smiled, nonetheless.

"I will admit that I had some fun with it, but you know what I can offer you, so let's get down to business."

"Business?"

"Yes. What do you want?"

"What makes you think I want anything from you?"

"Let us not be absurd now, Felix. You sought me out for a reason."

In film studies, there is a wonderful term that encompasses a range of circumstances and emotions in a viewer – suspension of disbelief. When you settle down to watch a film, you need to accept the rules of the world presented to you by the film in order to have a fruitful experience. If monsters appear, you need to suspend your disbelief of monsters, and understand that they form part of the world you are choosing to experience at that moment. If you dismiss them as fictional creatures, you are doing yourself a huge disservice as a viewer and will most likely not enjoy the film.

Felix did not believe in the supernatural. He firmly rejected the possibility of the existence of God or Satan and viewed the ideas of heaven and hell as ludicrous. He felt sorry for people who went through life expecting posthumous rewards for good behavior and fearing punishment for the contrary. The system of rewards and punishment was dealt out to the living, and it was far from fair. There was no afterlife to either look forward to or be afraid of. After you died, there was nothing left. No body. No soul. Nothing.

Firm in his belief that no actual consequences would result from pursuing a conversation with his own reflection in the mirror, Felix decided to play along. If you are having a dream where you are about the enjoy the sensual pleasures of Aishwarya Rai, you do not stop yourself and consider the illogical probability of this ever happening, you just go with it. On the other hand, if he was simply losing his mind, it wouldn't matter either. After all, people who are insane do not actually know they are insane, do they? Ignorance is bliss.

"Yes. I summoned you," answered Felix, fully embracing the unnatural situation. "I want a complete body makeover. Six-Pack. Muscles. Strong jaw. The works."

The reflection simply stared at Felix with a cruel look that was a combination of amusement and disdain.

Felix continued with his list. "No excessive sweating, but no dry skin either, you know, a good balance. Also, nice, straight white teeth that would put Britney Spears' smile to shame." He paused for a moment and considered. "Are you going to remember all this? There's more."

"I do not need a laundry list, my friend. It is enough for you to desire it with intensity. Envision it in your mind, and it will happen – for a price, of course."

"Of course," replied Felix nonchalantly. "So, when will I

know this is actually happening?"

"Oh, you will know. You can be sure of that," answered the reflection in the mirror, and with those ominous words lost its independence, and went back to be a natural reflection that replicated Felix's movements.

"I missed you at the shoot yesterday," a slightly hoarse voice came from behind him.

Felix recognized the young man from Sweet Cherry Productions he had met in the same place the day before. He was dressed the same, but this time his youthful good looks were not as striking. He had dark circles under his eyes, and the beginning of crow's feet on the sides. His long mane of golden hair was still there but seemed a bit thinner and somewhat faded and Felix thought he could see the beginning of a belly starting to form under the cinched robe. Felix could not suppress a tiny gasp of surprise.

"What happened to you?"

"Rough day," the young man answered sadly. "It all catches up to you, you know. Don't forget that."

Felix was about to ask him what he meant, but the young man just turned around and walked away without a word, dragging his feet as he left the restroom. *Whatever*, Felix thought to himself and left as well.

After arriving at his apartment that night, Felix checked his reflection in the mirror at least one hundred times until the early hours of the morning. He was not sure what he was expecting, but whatever it was, it was not happening, so he gave up and went to sleep, chiding himself for his naivete.

About an hour later, a gnawing pain in his gums woke Felix up. This was not necessarily uncommon. He had felt it before and had had several issues with oral health throughout his life.

"Fucking Brit ancestors," he muttered as he made his way to the bathroom mirror. As he examined his mouth, he noticed that his gums were redder and more enflamed than he had ever seen them. His teeth also felt loose and when he touched one of them, it fell right into the sink in front of him. It was soon followed by the rest of them that fell like grotesque, tiny hail stones from his mouth accompanied by bloody clumps that he could only guess were pieces of his gums.

Horrified, Felix went for a towel to staunch the bleeding, but as soon as his fingers touched it, his nails started blackening and falling off as well. Felix looked around wildly, and grabbed his head in terror, only to find bloody patches of hair and skin attached to his hands. Unable to escape from this nightmare, Felix cried out, but the sound of his voice was drowned out by loud, cracking and popping noises. The bones in his entire body were breaking of their own accord, and his sinews and muscles were being pulled in every direction, ripping apart his flesh and exposing his internal organs. The body that had once belonged to Felix was literally falling to pieces. Within minutes it was reduced to a throbbing, pulsating, unrecognizable mass and soon afterwards, it throbbed and pulsated no more.

Britney applied make-up in front of her dresser mirror and was pleased with what she saw. All her life she had been told that she was pretty, and she was fully aware of the fact that it was true. Internally, she suffered from no false modesty, but the confidence she projected from her beauty was far from aggressive and in fact, was perceived as somehow unknown to her, which, of course, made her even more attractive.

Britney was the type of person who was constantly hounded because of her looks. There were days that she had to turn down one invitation after another, from both men and women, trying to get closer to her by asking her out. Although it became irritating at times, she always did so with respect and even kindness, citing her exclusive relationship with her boyfriend as the reason. In this way, those that respected monogamy would back off and those who did not felt that if the boyfriend was not an obstacle, they would have a shot with Britney.

For Britney, being in a committed relationship was a good excuse to give others, but she often wondered if she herself was as convinced about it deep, down inside. Her boyfriend was an officer in the Marines and was rarely in New York. When he was in town, they were inseparable, and the romance was as passionate as the ones that are narrated in the Harlequin novels. However, once he left, the feeling of emptiness was tremendous, and Britney asked herself if the whole thing was even worth it. She was not naïve enough to think that a handsome, young marine spent entire weeks, or even months on end staring at a photograph of her, and she had gone out on a few casual dates with other men herself during the two years of their relationship, but, as ignorance is bliss, neither of them ever talked about it, so it was like it had never happened.

Lately, Britney had decided to announce that she was in a relationship as a sort of preemptive strike to let everyone know that she was unavailable. The strategy had mixed results, but at least her conscience was clear. There was one person, though, with which she had not done this. Her new supervisor, Felix, did not know that she had a boyfriend, and if he did, she had not been the one to tell him. Felix was a strange sort. He was a complete gentleman and friendly, although shy. He was good-looking but could use some time at the gym. Also, his general demeanor was so self-conscious and awkward that any attractiveness he had, could be easily lost in the first few minutes of meeting him. Nevertheless, Britney was drawn to him, as someone might be to a piece of art that is rough around the edges but has the potential to become a masterpiece.

She was not quite sure how to approach the situation, though. During the training sessions, she had dropped a few hints, a hair-flip here, an eyelash bat there, a flirty tap on the shoulder here and there – but nothing. Most men would have already been making motel reservations at this point, but not Felix. He was either completely clueless, brilliant at appearing clueless, or gay. Whichever the case, she intended to make a clear move today. It would have to be something that even someone like Felix could not ignore. She was not sure what she would do, but she knew that if it did not work, he was definitely not interested.

Unfortunately for Britney, her resolve in the matter amounted to nothing as Felix did not show up to work that day, nor the day after, nor the day after that. After a week-long absence, employees at the company were informed that Felix Dupont was taking some time off due to personal reasons and would not be back for several weeks. It was a full three months before Britney saw Felix again, and when she finally did, it was almost as though she were meeting him for the first time.

The receptionist at Professional Document Services fiddled with her new smart phone. Her bright, multicolored fingernails danced over the shiny keypad and she was enthralled in the world of online gossip when she heard a deep, masculine voice say, "Good morning."

Without even bothering to look up, and in a tone that denoted exasperation at being interrupted, she answered, "Help you?"

"My pass key doesn't seem to be working. Could you please

buzz me in?"

Having moved on to Tinder, she was now swiping left and right on her phone.

"Name?"

"Felix Dupont."

The receptionist looked up, and a gasp of excitement escaped her. In front of her was a beautiful man who seemed to have stepped out of a GQ magazine. He was the cliched tall, dark, and handsome type with a smile that lit up the room and eyes that seemed to look straight into your soul. She sat up straighter and adjusted her blouse, making sure that Felix caught an eyeful of her cleavage before saying, "Hi. I'm Gloria."

"Yes. I know, Gloria. We've met before. I... took some time off."

"Are you sure?" asked Gloria. "I think I would have remembered that," she added, flashing a seductive smile.

"I'm sure," replied Felix. "I guess I'm just not that memorable."

Gloria just kept on staring at Felix as if salivating over a juicy piece of steak instead of speaking to a human being.

"Gloria?" Felix said, leaning in close to Gloria and staring into her large, heavily made-up eyes.

"Yes?" cooed Gloria, melting at the sound of her own name in the mouth of such a gorgeous man, and foolishly expecting to be kissed.

"I have work to do," said Felix and motioned toward the buzzer with his eyes.

"Right. Sorry!" exclaimed Gloria, snapping back into reality as she pressed the buzzer. "Hey, maybe later we can..." she started to say, but Felix was already through the door.

"Wow!" she sighed and started to dial the extensions of her

friends at the company to spread the news about the hot new guy at the company.

The small company was abuzz with the return of Felix. Nobody knew (or cared) about why he had been gone so long. The chatter was all about how different (and good) he looked. Felix took it all in stride. He fully enjoyed all the appreciative looks he got and seemed much more comfortable with small talk than anyone had ever seen him before. After more than a few double takes, people accepted that this incredibly attractive man was indeed Felix Dupont who had returned to work.

Felix made his way to the Quality Control area where Britney was now established in her position after having completed the three-month probation period. He saw her looking over some newly scanned documents and simply said, "Hey, you. Remember me?"

Britney looked at Felix in stupefaction. "Oh, my God! Felix, you look so…"

"Different?" offered Felix.

"You look great. Welcome back."

She moved closer to Felix as if to hug him but caught herself in time.

"Thanks," answered Felix as he looked at Britney steadily.

This made Britney a bit uncomfortable, but not necessarily in a bad way.

"So… you're back. What happened?" she asked imprudently, immediately regretting her words. "I'm sorry, Felix. It's none of my business."

Felix looked at her with sad eyes but said in a firm voice, "That's fine, Britney. I'll tell you all about it tonight over drinks."

Although it was a clear statement, Britney was taken by surprise, and could only ask, "Drinks?"

"8.00 p.m. at Harrigan's. See you then."

He then flashed her a confident smile full of straight, white teeth, and left without giving her a chance to say anything else.

Britney did not know what to think. Although she had made the resolution to explore her possibilities with Felix three months ago, she always assumed that she would be in the driver's seat. Felix's lack of confidence was something she had planned to use to her advantage in the event of a potential relationship. Her Marine boyfriend was very much a take-charge sort of man, perhaps because of his military lifestyle, and that was one of the things that most attracted her to him, but she was certainly not expecting the same attitude from Felix, and that perplexed her. Nonetheless, she was intrigued. This new-and-improved Felix was certainly a bonus, and she was genuinely glad to see him again. Drinks at Harrigan's sounded like a wonderful plan.

Britney arrived at Harrigan's at five minutes to eight. She scolded herself for this social faux pax as she did not want to appear overeager, but relaxed when she saw that Felix was already waiting for her at a table, strategically placed in a corner for privacy. Once the initial awkwardness of a first encounter, which is somewhere between friendship and romance, was out of the way, the conversation between Britney and Felix flowed very easily, and Britney felt happier than she had in a long time. This might actually work out. Britney told herself and was surprised at just how much she wanted it to. Felix was charming. He made all the right gestures and said all the right things.

He opened up to her about how his extended absence had been due to a nervous breakdown, and that the changes in his physical appearance and demeanor were just due to the fact that he had had three months in which to reflect and decide to take charge of his life. Britney has too hypnotized by the moment to analyze the logic of the explanation Felix was giving her for such an extreme transformation. She was focused on his long eyelashes, his strong jawline, the firm yet tender way in which he held her hand. She watched his lips moving and was certain that soon they would be pressed against hers. In fact, if he as much as suggested they spend the night together, she would have no qualms whatsoever. She was ready, willing, and desirous of giving herself over completely to Felix if he wanted her, and she hoped mind, body and soul that he did.

All of Felix's suffering was about to pay off. He could see in Britney's eyes that she wanted him, and he was moments away from turning his fantasy into reality. The physical pain of his transformation had been excruciating. His body had been reduced to a shapeless mass on his bathroom floor three months ago, but he had been fully conscious of what was happening to him, unable to see as he had no eyes and unable to scream as he had no mouth. After what had seemed like an eternity, the unrecognizable remains of what was once Felix Dupont started rearranging themselves within what appeared to be a massive clump of clay. The obscene spectacle was one worth of the Grand Guignol as bone, flesh and fluids started randomly coming together to form a grotesque semblance of a human being.

There seemed to be no method to the unnatural process. An eye popped up where a knee should be, a hand sprouted forth from behind a shoulder blade, and a heart manifested itself where one would expect to see a face. Organs would shift position, becoming larger and smaller. It was the stuff of nightmares. After hours of indescribable pain, the unseen demonic force behind this danse macabre seemed to gain an understanding of human anatomy, and Felix Dupont was once again whole.

Although supposedly an atheist, Felix understood perfectly

well that dark forces were at play here. If he were reluctant to give them a name, he could not deny their existence and obvious power. He had wanted a complete physical transformation, and he had gotten it. A few hours of physical pain were a small price to pay for what were bound to be phenomenal results. He looked at the mirror to see his new body, but the only thing that greeted him was the reflection of his own face filled with fury. He looked exactly the same. Everything he had put himself through had been for naught. He screamed at the mirror with all his might, demanding an explanation, but it was useless.

Suddenly, he remembered that this had happened before. He could not communicate with just any mirror. It had to be the eighth-floor mirror in the building where he worked. Throwing on a long, hooded coat and exiting his own building like a madman, Felix rushed to Professional Document Services and entered the familiar restroom. If never a pleasant space to begin with, the restroom was now in a more disgusting state than ever. The walls and floor were grimy to the touch. The toilets and urinals were overflowing with human waste. The stench was unbearable, and the mirrors were so cracked that each reflection was deformed and multiplied by a thousand.

Everything around him was a dire warning to leave. Anyone in his right mind would look at the surroundings and do just that, regardless of any belief in the supernatural. Felix did not leave. He was here to get answers and he would get them – at any cost.

"Hey!" he yelled at the mirror. "What the fuck?" Show yourself! I'm going to tear this entire fucking dump apart until you talk to me."

Nothing. He started punching and kicking everything in sight. Most of the hardware holding things together was rusted to the core, so this did not take long. A series of kicks brought down the wall of the first stall which in turn brought down the rest of them in a thunderous domino effect. A few hearty pulls ripped the sinks off the wall in a shower of broken tiles. Felix broke off a rusted pipe and started going at the light fixtures. Decades-old wiring came apart as sparks flew throughout the room. Still nothing.

Felix caught a glimpse of his maniacal reflection in the mirror, and pipe in hand, poised himself to throw it with all his might.

"Do not do it," his reflection finally spoke up.

The voice was steady, but Felix thought he could detect a slight trace of fear in it.

"Or what?" asked Felix defiantly.

"Or you will not get what you want."

"I already didn't get what I wanted."

"Do not be foolish, Felix. You are so close. Do not throw it all away when you are so close. After all you have been through."

"Exactly! After all I've been through…" Felix was close to tears, "…everything is exactly the same."

"You did not honestly think it would be that simple, did you? Everything has a price and I have not yet named mine."

"I told you that I would do anything."

"Yes. Indeed. Your word is your bond and all that, but I am going to need something in writing."

"Writing? You mean like a goddamn contract?" asked Felix in stupefaction.

"A *God-damned* contract," repeated the reflection, placing special emphasis on the compound-adjective. "Yes. That is exactly what I mean. Excellent choice of words."

Given the circumstances, and the lack of appropriate business setting with the accompanying writing implements,

Felix removed a shard of glass from the mirror, cut open the palm of his hand, and smeared Felix Dupont on the mirror in front of him.

"There is no turning back now, friend," said a trembling, elderly voice behind him.

Felix turned around him, and once again saw the familiar Sweet Cherry Productions logo, except now the wearer was a sickly, haggard, decrepit, old man with sunken eyes, yellow skin, and blackened teeth. His remaining gray hair fell in thin strands framing a face with profound sorrow and pain etched in every wrinkle.

"No turning back," the old man repeated as enormous tears fell down his exhausted face.

He then drooped his head down in defeat and simply faded into nothingness. It did not take an advanced degree in paranormal studies to figure out what this meant. Felix realized that this apparition had tried to warn him, albeit in a typical, non-productive, non-effective manner as is commonly seen in horror films. Surely, he had made his own blood boon, and was now paying for the consequences of his acts. Notwithstanding all evidence to the contrary, Felix refused to believe that he would share the same fate and rushed back to his apartment to wait.

During the next month, the same thing happened to Felix every single night. The complete destruction of his body followed by the chaotic reconstruction of the same. The only difference was that now, after suffering the grueling process every day, he would be rewarded with something aesthetically pleasing – flat abdomen, muscular thighs, flawless skin. He had grown used to the routine, dreading the pain, but anxious to reap the benefits, until one night, Felix looked at himself in a full-length mirror, and for the first time in his life, was completely satisfied with what he saw. From that moment on, the transformations stopped.

He had been using his accrued sick time at Professional Document Services. Luckily, he had plenty of it, but, according to company policy, after twelve weeks he could lose his job, and four had already passed. On the other hand, he could not just waltz into work out of the blue looking like he did. He decided that a medical leave was the way to go. He would claim a mental health crisis, and the new-and-improved body would be the result of intense physical therapy on his road to recovery. It was certainly flimsy as far as logical explanations went, but it would have to do. Two months later, he was sitting at Harrigan's with the gorgeous Britney staring lovingly at him.

This was one of those rare moments where everything seems to fall into place. Felix and Britney made a nice couple. Felix was ready for a relationship and Britney, although technically in one already, had firmly decided in her mind to end things with the Marine and explore the wonderful possibilities with Felix. Felix leaned in remarkably close to Britney so that their faces were within kissing distance. He had once seen in an old black-and-white film from the thirties that a very dapper and debonair gentleman had used the line 'So where do we go from here?' on his lady friend, and had been rewarded with a kiss, so he figured he would try it. What came out instead was, "Poor jarhead, putting his ass on the line, so that his slut girlfriend can step out on him."

It took Britney a moment to realize what she had just heard as her eyes were half closed, and she was fully enjoying the romantic moment, but when she finally did, it was like a bucket of ice water thrown in her face.

"Excuse me?" she said, anger and indignation dominating

her voice.

Felix was just as shocked or even more so than Britney at his own words. He searched desperately for an appropriate apology in his mind, but his actual words were, "I mean, I realize that all women are cheating whores, but a Marine is an American hero. You would think that his standards were above a common streetwalker like you."

Britney could not think of a single retort. Instead, she burst into tears and managed a single word between sobs before storming out of Felix's life forever.

"Asshole!"

Felix's brain ordered him to yell 'Wait!' but what came out was, *"Skank!"*

What on earth was happening to him? Why could he not control his own words? It was as if someone were speaking through him. He threw a wad of bills on the table without bothering to check their denomination and raced out of Harrigan's. Most patrons assumed that he would go after the beautiful blonde that had just run out, but Britney was the furthest thing from Felix's mind now. He needed answers, and he knew just where to get them.

Felix entered the dreaded restroom for the last time on this plane of existence. It no longer resembled a room. Objects were no longer recognizable, and the stench of death and decay permeated every pore in Felix's body. The only thing that Felix could clearly make out was his own reflection in the mirror that was now spotless. What he saw reflected was his ideal of masculine beauty. He recognized something of Felix Dupont in the image, but he also realized that he had lost his way long before his encounter with the mirror.

He had rejected the ideas of good and evil as fanatical

nonsense without understanding that his adamant refusal to believe in anything would ultimately be his demise. He allowed vanity to take over his existence and did not measure the consequences of feeding his desire to become something he was never meant to be. Felix stared at his reflection that was now beckoning him to join it. Stubborn and unbelieving until the bitter end, he threw himself headlong into the mirror which swallowed him whole before shattering into a million pieces. *What do I have to lose?* Felix asked himself as he disappeared into his own reflection, but he knew the answer. He had lost everything.

The Little Things

Malcolm observed the woman in front of him with great interest. Some time ago, he had almost completely tuned out what she was saying to concentrate on her facial expressions and the movement of her body. Of course, every now and then, he would tune in to catch key phrases. This would allow him to nod and offer slight reactions in all the right places. So far, he had heard most of the played-out classics: my boyfriend, does not get me, something spontaneous, accompanied by some newer ones that that would very soon make it into the realm of classics: experiment, girlfriends, threesome. These fragments had been spread out during two hours of conversation, or rather monologue, if you considered the fact that Malcolm had barely opened his mouth at all.

There was a relatively simple storyline here with a narrow margin of error. Malcolm's dinner companion had been in a serious relationship for many years. Her boyfriend was older, and presumably wiser, although Malcolm wondered about the latter. He was apparently a very responsible, dependable, and stable man, which, of course, was a turn-off for a young woman in her position. She needed someone dark and mysterious that would sweep her off her feet and make her feel alive. *It would also be a plus if he treated her like garbage*, Malcolm added as an afterthought. Because he had not been listening carefully to the words, he was not quite sure where the threesome fit in, but it was probably one of three possibilities: 1. The boyfriend agreed to a threesome with another woman. This seemed logical enough. 2. The boyfriend refused a threesome with another woman. This seemed highly unlikely to Malcolm, although he supposed it was a possibility. 3. She was throwing the term out there to peak Malcolm's interest. The latter seemed the most plausible. In any event, it did not matter to Malcolm. He had already decided he would have sex with…? Malcolm searched his brain for the young woman's name but could not find it.

"Listen… you. Hold that thought, and I'll be right back."

He gave her a sly smile and headed to the restroom. She returned a sexy smile and took a sip of her drink. Malcolm did not look back at his date as he headed toward the restroom. That is exactly what she would expect him to do. He entered the restroom and looked at himself in the mirror. Truth be told, Malcolm was not much to look at. He was a large man, standing six-feet-five-inches tall, and weighing two hundred and fifty pounds. His hair was visibly thinning on top, and he had pasty, white skin. He was not the best dresser either. He wore brown, corduroy pants, a too-large blazer with cheap sneakers and tube socks that he had picked up at the local dollar store. Malcolm splashed water on his face, and slicked back what remained of his hair. He stared at his reflection, revealing what was perhaps his most attractive feature. He had big, beautiful, piercing, black eyes with an intensity to them that was difficult to describe, and the accompanying long eyelashes to go with them. This unique characteristic almost singlehandedly made up for the rest of his physical shortcomings and is what seemingly drew beautiful women to Malcolm in a considerably steady flow.

Of course, his eyes would only serve a decorative purpose if it were not for his overwhelming self-confidence that did not quite wander into the realm of cockiness. Malcolm knew plenty of men with sculptural physiques, and flawless features that did not get the time of day from women due to their lack of self-confidence. Malcolm returned to his date and resumed his mission of conquest. As if she had been on pause during his absence, the young woman waited for him to sit down, and continued her monologue.

"So, my boyfriend says to me, Gina, don't play innocent with me…"

Gina. That's her name. Malcolm made a mental note.

"… You know guys want to have sex with you when they see you, and you love it. Don't deny it. That's why you dress the way you do…" Gina continued. "I mean… what's wrong with how I dress?" Gina stood up, revealing skintight jeans, and a wife beater two sizes too small for her.

Malcolm just smiled politely. He did not care what she wore as long as she took it off very soon. Gina sat down after making sure that both Malcolm and the rest of the patrons at the restaurant had gotten an eyeful. She went on talking, and Malcolm tuned her out once again. She was undeniably an incredibly attractive woman. Malcolm had once read the writer, Madeline L'Engle, describe a woman's beauty as an assault. This was very appropriate for the woman he had in front of him. Gina was overtly sensual, and her whole demeanor oozed raw sexuality. She was half Cuban and half Korean, which gave her the perfect combination of voluptuous Latin curves and exotic Asian features. Malcolm suddenly felt guilty about what he was planning to do. He was going to bed the trophy whore of some poor slob that was probably not only paying for her cell phone and birth control, but for this dinner as well. Somehow it felt wrong, but he knew that if he did not do it, someone else would, and he could not miss out on such an opportunity.

What followed was something that, seen through outside eyes, would have been condemned as a date killer. Without even bothering to let her finish her sentence, Malcolm yawned loudly, and cut her off rudely.

"Time to go, Gina."

Gina did not believe what she had just seen happen. Although she knew well that most men just stared at her chest for the duration of the conversation, they at least pretended to pay attention to what she was saying. She frowned at Malcolm because she figured it was the expected reaction, but she was not really angry. This man intrigued her.

"Come on, sweetness. Lay out the Benjamins, so we can blow this pop stand," he said, distractedly pointing to her purse.

She gave him a perfunctory huff as she fished around for the money.

"You know…" she said, "… a gentleman would not expect a lady to pay on their first time out together."

Malcolm simply chuckled.

"Yeah, well, a lady would actually wear underwear on her first date with a guy, so I guess we're even."

No one had ever talked to Gina like this before. She felt hot anger rush to her cheeks, but she could not help feeling a surge of excitement at the same time. Was this guy for real? He certainly had a brass pair on him, but she would not play his game. She could not show him how she truly felt. Instead, she opened her eyes wide in a mock expression of wonder.

"Date? Is that what you think this is?"

Malcolm replied smugly.

"You can worry about the semantics if it floats your boat. It's all the same to me."

He waited for her to put the money on the table, and then

grabbed her by the hand firmly, without quite being rough, and led her to the exit. He looked like a poor lumberjack in his Sunday best accompanied by a hip, young model from a glossy urban magazine. It was quite the picture to behold.

What followed were three hours in a cheap motel room, also paid for by Gina, or perhaps her generous boyfriend. After going several rounds, they were both exhausted. Despite his looks, Malcolm was quite the lover. He was determined, passionate, and drove the women he was with to near hysteria on many occasions.

Malcolm sat on the edge of the bed getting dressed while Gina was in the shower. He always liked to shower before the woman. This way, he would be dressed by the time she came out and say that he had to leave. He was never a fan of the post-act conversation. He was especially not in the mood for it at this hour of the night. He realized that having sex with a co-worker was probably a mistake. He did not really care what people thought, but he did not like socializing in the workplace, and what had just happened gave Gina an excuse to talk to him at work. Whatever her thoughts were, he did not want to hear them. The cliches annoyed him terribly, and women were full of them, especially after sex. *Where is this going?* or *This was a mistake.* Either end of the spectrum proved indigestible to Malcolm because of its blatant untruth and latent hypocrisy. There was one phrase, though, that made his blood curdle. "If she says to me …" he started to say aloud but was interrupted by the bathroom door opening.

Gina was quite a sight, standing there, dripping water, with only a towel covering her smoldering body. She let the towel drop ceremoniously to the floor. She walked over to Malcolm, kissed the top of his head, and completed the thought he had begun just moments ago. "I don't know what happened to me with you, Malcolm. I don't usually do this type of thing."

What happened next only took a couple of seconds. Quick as a cat, Malcolm stood up, snapped Gina's neck, and sat back down on the bed. He was already sitting when her gorgeous, lifeless body crumpled to the floor. Yes, it was a rash action. he admitted to himself. She certainly did not deserve to die because of a phrase that annoyed him, but Malcolm could not help it. It was always the little things that got to him. It was always the little things that made him mad.

Malcolm sat at his cubicle typing away. He displayed no discernible expression on his face but seemed to be looking at something beyond the computer screen that only he could see. It had been two months since he had gone out with Gina. She had already faded from everyone's memory. Nobody even knew that she was dead. For the first couple of days that she did not show up, there had been some talk about the hot girl who had not even lasted a week, but by the third day, it was old news. It was not at all uncommon for employees not to return to work after a few days on the job at the company where Malcolm worked. All the department managers knew this, and they figured it into their budgets.

The high turnover rate brought in a slew of new faces constantly, and made anonymity quite easy, which suited Malcolm fine. Most new employees were recent high school graduates, or college dropouts. There was also a wide variety of artists in almost every field that needed a bullshit, pay-the-rent job while pursuing their creative endeavors, and several lifers who had been there for decades too. Malcolm was still too young to fit into the last category, but he was certainly on his way. It had been his first job out of college, and he would be reaching the twelve-year mark soon. Although quite intelligent, Malcolm was not a particularly ambitious man. As long as he had food and shelter, he was basically content. He had no desire to look for another job and planned to stay there until he either dropped dead or was kicked out.

A monkey could carry out Malcolm's job, provided it had motor and mental skills that were slightly above average. When he was first hired, over a decade ago, he had swelled with pride at his newfound title: Commercial Identification Specialist for the Media Research Division. Wow! That was a tall order for a recent college graduate. Now, twelve years later, he had the same position which consisted of doing the following: The company recorded twenty-four hours a day of television and radio programming.

Malcolm's job was to go through these tapes and find new advertising spots. He would fast forward through the actual programming, and then check each spot against the company database. If it already existed there, he would move on to the next one. If not, he would write a short description of it, and add it to the database. That was the extent of his duties. Among his peers, which consisted of another two dozen scanners, as they were commonly called, he was something of an intellectual. Apparently proper spelling, grammar, and punctuation were considered rare qualities at this company. Because of this, Malcolm's supervisor, a lifer, who was reaching the thirty-year mark, basically left Malcolm alone, and gave him the special distinction of being the only employee in the division who never had to work overnights, weekends, or holidays.

Malcolm worked the second shift, from 4.00 p.m. until midnight, so he had most of the day free, but he did not really take advantage of his free time. He would sleep in every day and treat himself to a large breakfast at the local diner. At about 3.00 p.m., he would go back to the same diner and have a smaller meal. Then it was time for work. After work, he would sometimes walk around Times Square and observe the people around him. Occasionally, he would hook up with some random woman for the night. Otherwise, he would just go to his rent-controlled apartment on the Lower East Side and go through the same routine all over again.

Malcolm finished typing up the last description of the day and turned off his computer. He said good night to no one in particular, never expecting a reply and rarely getting one, and left the office. The building was half a block away from the subway station, and he was tired, so he decided to go straight home. On the train, he was lucky enough to find a seat, and took it. New York was the only place Malcolm knew of that would have a packed subway car after midnight in the middle of the week. He liked to observe the people on the train, but he was careful to do it very subtly. This city was full of psychos, and on more than one occasion, people who did not like to be looked at, had threatened him. He was just about to begin his observation, when two black, teenage boys carrying boxes of candy bars came in from the next car with a loud greeting.

"Good evening, ladies and gentlemen!" one of them began.

There were several eye rolls, and audible sighs among the passengers. Everybody already knew what was coming up. The young man continued.

"Can we have your attention please? My name is Darnell, and this is my associate, Tyrone."

Associate? Malcolm thought to himself. Were these kids part of a law firm? They could not be more than fifteen years old. He prepared himself for the routine. The same youth continued speaking, while his associate stood by moving his body to a tune that only he could hear. Perhaps he was a silent partner.

"We is here tonight selling candy. Not for no church. Not for no basketball team. We is here, so we can have money in our pockets, get a education, and stay out of trouble."

Malcolm cringed at the speech pattern. These kids *were* in desperate need of education, if only to improve their grammar. Speaking of which, what were they doing out so late on a school night? And where were their parents?

"White people, you have nothing to fear. We is just a couple of brothers trying to keep it real," continued the eloquent speaker.

This really hit a nerve in Malcolm. Why was it that Caucasians were always an acceptable target for racial jokes, while so-called minorities were untouchable? He felt a vein in his right temple begin to throb painfully, but he tried to remain calm. The young man spoke some more nonsense about oppression, Mother Africa, and beating the system. Malcolm observed the two young men carefully. Their thick, gold chains and two-hundred-dollar sneakers did not make them appear to be particularly oppressed. He was willing to bet that neither of them had ever been anywhere near Africa in their lives and would probably have trouble locating it on a map. As far as beating the system, milking the system was more like it. Malcolm was very irritated by now.

The silent partner finally spoke. "And remember..." he added as a conclusion to his friend's monologue, "any donation you make tonight will keep us out of the courthouse and *your* house."

He made special emphasis on the penultimate word and pointed to a group of passengers on the train, all of them white, who seemed to deem this the funniest thing in the world and laughed heartily. This set Malcolm off. Was he supposed to be grateful to these punks for not robbing him? What if he did not *feel* like giving them a fucking penny? Would it then be his fault if they stole from him in the future?

"Shut up, you fucking idiots," he said angrily as he stood up. The two young men turned around defensively, but relaxed when they realized that Malcolm was talking to the crowd of laughing people who quickly became silent. A man of Malcolm's size could be quite intimidating when he was mad. Malcolm moved closer to them.

"Can't you see that these two losers are a pair of manipulative scumbags?"

The young man who had spoken first said, "Hey! Who you calling scumbag, cracker?"

Malcolm turned to him, eyes glowering, and the youth took a reflexive step back. By this time, several passengers had already moved closer to the exit doors but were watching the exchange with interest. Malcolm moved in on the two teenagers and said very slowly.

"How is it that you can use the word *cracker*, and get away with it, while if I even think the word *nigger,* it becomes a drama of national proportions?"

Both teens reacted violently upon hearing the term used, and with the carelessness of youth that does not consider consequences, attempted a futile attack on Malcolm. One of them received the full force of a backhand slap from Malcolm right across the face. He was literally airborne for a few seconds, and then crashed painfully back first into a pole. The other one got Malcolm's boot in the center of the chest. The force was so strong that instead of falling on his back, his legs went out from behind him, and he fell flat on his face. At this precise moment, the subway doors opened, and a car that had been full only moments ago, was empty in less than five seconds. Both boys staggered to their feet in a daze and tried to run out the same door simultaneously. Malcolm simply grabbed them both by the back of their shirts and pulled them back into the car. He was not quite finished yet. Several new passengers took a few steps inside the car, saw what was happening, and exited immediately. You could always count on New Yorkers to look the other way when trouble was brewing. The subway cars closed again, and the train continued its route.

In the two minutes it took the train to reach the next station, Malcolm went to work on his victims. The sounds of breaking bones, torn flesh and desperate cries were drowned out by the train's engine speeding through the underground tunnels of the city.

It is important to remember that every single car in the New York City subway system comes equipped with intercoms that connect directly to the conductor's cabin, which in turn, is connected to the police department. Despite this nifty security system, Malcolm had plenty of time to beat two young men to death between stations and simply exited the train at the next station without ever seeing an officer of the law. The story made the next morning's news, but, as usual in this type of case, nobody had seen or heard anything. Malcolm had not really wanted to kill the teens, but it was always the little things that made him lose control. The little things were always problematic.

Several months after the subway incident, Malcolm was shopping for groceries at the mini market. Markets in Manhattan were always crowded. The time did not matter. This was truly the city that never slept. Malcolm took his shopping basket up to the counter, but, before he could make it there, a fat lady with about a million shades of red hair blocked him with the front of her shopping cart. She offered him a stupid smile that said *Better luck next time, chump.* Malcolm could have very easily pushed past her, but he was not in the mood for a confrontation, so he simply took a step back. The woman wedged her blubbery body through the narrow space between checkout counters, pulling the cart behind her. Malcolm waited patiently as the woman unloaded her cart. When the cart was empty, she just left it there, and turned her attention toward the cashier. Malcolm felt fire rushing through his veins. She obviously had no intention of moving it, so if he wanted to reach the checkout, he would either have to ask her to move it or move it himself. Once again, he struggled to keep his composure, but his voice trembled slightly when he spoke.

"Ma'am, you forgot to move your cart."

The woman faced him for a moment and gave him the same stupid smile as before then turned away again. She either did not understand him or was pretending not to. He turned to the cashier for help, but she was examining her fingernails and apparently could not be bothered with trivialities such as customer service. Malcolm swallowed his anger and moved the cart out of the way himself. Neither the lady nor the cashier even glanced in his direction. The woman's total was close to two hundred dollars, and the cashier repeated it to her three times, each time louder than the previous one. There was obviously a language barrier here. It had always seemed odd to Malcolm how some people thought that repeating an unknown language at a higher volume would magically translate it for a person who was not familiar with it. After fishing through her purse for what seemed like an eternity, the woman finally pulled out a welfare card. The cashier took it without emotion and tried unsuccessfully to scan it several times before handing it back to the woman unceremoniously.

"You don't go no money on it, lady," she said with an unmistakable New York Latina accent.

"What you mean is no money? Is credit card from government!" the woman replied indignantly. She had an extraordinarily strong Eastern European accent.

The cashier looked mildly annoyed. "That is not no credit card. That is a welfare card. You have to have it activated by the welfare office, or else it don't work."

By this time, Malcolm was sweating bullets. He felt blood rushing to his head.

"I want see manager. This no good. I want see manager now," the woman demanded.

Now the cashier was angry too. "This don't got nothing to do with the manager. He's going to tell you exactly the same thing."

"I want see manager," the woman insisted.

The cashier rolled her eyes, and, without moving a muscle, called out at the top of her lungs, *"Jose!"*

Malcolm suddenly found himself wondering if glamor school should be a prerequisite for all customer service positions. A young, Hispanic man in his early twenties joined them. He was not much older than the cashier, but he was clean cut and looked very professional in a nice, two-piece suit. *Jose will take care of this*, Malcolm thought confidently.

"What seems to be the trouble, ma'am?" Jose asked the fat lady very politely.

"She don't understand…" the cashier began, but Jose held up an authoritative hand.

"Let the customer speak, Clarisa."

Malcolm was impressed. Why couldn't there be more people like this young man in the world?

The red-haired lady started prattling on and on as Jose nodded attentively. Some of it sounded like English, but most of it seemed to be some strange, extraterrestrial language that only Jose could understand. Perhaps minimarket managers underwent some special training in angry-customer-speak. Jose let her finish, and then said, "I'm sorry, ma'am, but our policy here at City Market is that we do not accept inactive public assistance identification. If you care to wait a few minutes, I can call the office for you, and explain that you have a card that needs to be activated."

Malcolm was in awe of this pleasant young man. He was not only respectful, but kind as well. It was not his job to fix this stupid woman's problems. He was being more than accommodating. Notwithstanding, the woman began flailing her flabby arms around.

"I sue you! I sue she!" she screamed as she pointed first at Jose, and then at Clarisa. "I sue all supermarket!" she said, flapping her arms like a demented penguin.

"Ungrateful bitch!" Malcolm said aloud. In the few seconds that it took for her to turn around, and look at him, he thought, *If she gives me that stupid smile again…*

Sure enough, there it was, staring at him straight in the face, a taunting target, begging to be hit.

"Hmmm?" the woman said dreamily.

This was too much for Malcolm. He dropped his basket, grabbed her by the hair, and pulled her back into the battery display behind her. As many other times before, he underestimated his own strength. One of the metal hooks went straight through the back of her neck and came out her throat. A spray of blood shot out of her mouth and splattered the front of Clarisa's City Market vest. It took Clarisa a few moments to realize what had happened, but once she let out the first bloodcurdling scream, it spread through the entire minimarket like wildfire. Meanwhile, the unfortunate lady with the inactive welfare card stood there, impaled, gasping, and gurgling her final moments of life away. This was Malcolm's cue to leave. Nobody tried to stop him, but before he reached the exit, he heard a man's voice.

"Someone call 911."

Malcolm needed to clear his head. Why was it always the little things that made him react like this? He got on the first bus he could find without even checking its destination. It turned out the bus was going to Inwood. That could work out nicely. He would go to Inwood and walk around Fort Tryon Park. It was a nice place to relax. The bus had a lot of passengers for a Saturday morning, but Malcolm found an empty seat next to a well-dressed man in his early thirties. He had his legs spread wide open and was hunched over a newspaper. He gave Malcolm a quick glance but did not move.

"Excuse me," Malcolm said as he sat down next to him.

The man rustled his newspaper a bit and fidgeted a little in his seat, but made no real effort to give Malcolm any space. Malcolm decided that he would let this one go. Throughout the trip, Malcolm moved around in his seat to try to get into a more comfortable position, but the man reading the newspaper remained unfazed. He apparently could not take a hint. Just when Malcolm was going to resign himself to his uncomfortable seating arrangement, the man turned to him and said, "Hey, buddy. How about you quit rubbing up against me? It's very annoying."

Malcolm did not want to look at him for fear of doing something stupid out of anger, but answered him, nonetheless.

"Maybe you wouldn't have that problem if you closed your legs."

In response, the man opened his newspaper to a complete spread, rudely invading Malcolm's personal space. Malcolm's first impulse was to tear the paper away from him, and ram it down his throat, but he kept his cool. He had ended another life not twenty minutes ago. Two deaths in the same day would be too much, even for Malcolm. Instead, he took a deep breath, counted to ten, and let the air out slowly. This had worked for him before.

The driver announced the 207TH Street stop, and Malcolm got up, as did the well-dressed man, and a few others. Most passengers who got off at this stop were either going to the park or transferring to the A train. Malcolm hoped that the rude man with the newspaper had to catch the train. The idea of sharing an afternoon in the park with him made Malcolm sick to the stomach. Granted, *Fort Tryon Park* covered a large area. The probability that they would even see each other was slim to none, but Malcolm would *know* that he was somewhere. It was an extraordinarily little thing, but it bothered Malcolm intensely. It was always the little things that upset him.

Malcolm allowed the man to get off first, and waited for several others to pass him, so that there would be some distance between them. As luck would have it, they *were* both going to the park. The entrance closest to the bus stop was a double set of narrow stairs. Dozens of people went up and down the stairs by themselves, with their families, friends, or significant others. It was shaping up to be a gorgeous Saturday afternoon, and

Malcolm was feeling unusually happy. The stairs were divided by a thick, iron railing. Although there were no signs indicating direction, logic dictated that one side would be to ascend, and the other to descend. For the most part, people followed this unwritten rule, which allowed a smooth flow of pedestrian traffic. Malcolm spotted his ill-mannered bus mate up ahead on the stairs. Apparently, another well-dressed man coming down the stairs in the opposite direction spotted him as well, and yelled out, "Hey, Mike!"

Mike, who was not even remotely aware of how close he had come to being pummeled by Malcolm earlier, looked up.

"Billy! What's up?"

The two men shook hands over the railing and stopped to have a conversation. As soon as this happened, the flow of people lost its smoothness. These two inconsiderate assholes were chatting away in the middle of the stairs, oblivious to the great inconvenience they were causing everyone around them. Malcolm's nostrils flared like a raging bull. He had let Mike's lack of basic manners go unpunished before. He would not make the same mistake twice. Without any sort of preamble, he shot up the stairs and grabbed Mike by the armpit with one hand, and by the crotch with another. He then squatted down to gain strength and impulse, and lifted Mike straight over his head like a professional wrestler. Billy simply stared at him in horror as Mike wriggled with futility within Malcolm's powerful grip.

"What the fuck …?" were Mike's final words as Malcom body-slammed him viciously back first into the railing, producing the grotesque sound of a cracking spine.

Complete pandemonium broke out at this moment. Everyone started screaming and running in all directions in a desperate frenzy. Later that night, the evening news would report that several people had been trampled to death after witnessing a brutal murder. Panic settled in Malcolm's heart like a burning flash of pain, and he did what he had never done before. He ran. He ran as fast as his large frame could carry him. When it seemed that he had been running for hours and his lungs were straining for air, he stopped. He looked around him and saw that he was still somewhere inside the park. After he had rested a calmed down a bit, he started to wander. He wandered for hours, trying to make sense of everything that had happened. Two deaths within an hour of each other. This time, he had gone too far.

Malcolm had a high threshold for both physical and emotional pain. As a child, he had been beaten up frequently in school. He had always been tall, but as skinny as a pencil until reaching his early twenties when he had started to put on weight. Beatings by cruel schoolmates were usually complemented by beatings by his drunken father a couple of times a week, until the old man's liver had burst when Malcolm was fifteen. His mother had never remarried, but a string of her abusive lovers had taken his father's place until he had finally left home for college at eighteen. This had been fifteen years ago, but Malcolm was still tormented by feelings of shame for his cowardice. He had never once fought back. He would simply take the beatings and cry himself to sleep later. It was ironic that the fear of pain was what held him back from defending himself. He did not fight back because he was afraid of getting hurt, but by not fighting back, he got hurt much worse.

On the emotional side, he had been hurt a lot throughout his college years. When he met any girl, he would fall instantly in love with her until the inevitable heartbreak came when he realized the feeling was not reciprocal. When he made a new male friend, he thought he had found a blood brother that would be with him through thick and thin and was similarly disappointed when the superficiality of the friendship surfaced. All these things he suffered in silence, but the little things were bad. The little things made him go insane. If you broke Malcolm's nose, or tore his self-esteem to shreds, you were basically safe. However, if you made the mistake of cutting in front of him at the bank or leaving your clothes unattended at the laundromat after the wash cycle was finished, you would probably be in for a world of hurt.

Malcolm realized that it would begin to get dark soon. He would have to occupy himself with something, or all his wandering and thinking would give him brain fever soon. He noticed a very pretty, young woman sitting by herself on a bench. She had on a white sweater, and a black miniskirt with thigh-high, black, leather boots, revealing a small portion of unblemished, satiny, white skin. She was reading a book, and had bouncy, blonde hair that fell over her shoulders in cute, little curls.

Malcolm walked over and sat down beside her. She acknowledged his presence with a polite smile and went back to her reading. Malcolm decided he would go for it. He had no intention of trying to get her into bed. He would just strike up a conversation in a friendly manner with no ulterior motives. This would help get his mind off the day's events.

"This is a beautiful park, isn't it?" he began.

The woman looked up. "It sure is."

Malcolm detected a slight, Scandinavian accent. After a few moments of silence, she went back to her book.

"My name is Malcolm," he continued.

"Claudia," she answered, looking up once again.

Malcolm could tell that she was beginning to get annoyed by

the interruptions. He took the hint and remained silent for several minutes. Although it was not quite working out as he had hoped, it was not yet a lost cause. She probably thought that he was trying to pick her up, and though the prospect was not at all unpleasant to him, it was not his objective now. Malcolm thought it important to clarify this to her.

"Listen, Claudia…" he began, but before he could continue, Malcolm felt a sharp, hot pain in his throat.

It is common for time to be perceived differently during periods of great physical and emotional stress. What transpired took about five seconds, but what Malcolm saw was a slow-motion, frame-by-frame reel of his final moments in the world of the living. Claudia closed her eyes and shook her head disapprovingly from side to side. She slapped the book she was reading closed and threw it down angrily on the ground. She then opened her eyes and looked all around to make sure that the two of them were alone. Claudia unzipped a side pocket on one of her boots. From it she produced a shiny stiletto and stuck it mercilessly into Malcolm's jugular vein with amazing strength. Malcolm saw genuine hatred in her eyes, and died asking himself, *What happened?*

Claudia removed the stiletto from Malcolm's throat as easily as she had introduced it, ignoring the spray of blood that was now forming a pattern of dark spots on her pristine, white sweater. She knew that she had overreacted. He had not been at all disrespectful or vulgar toward her. Having been a victim of rape in the past, Claudia had learned to successfully read men's intentions. Malcolm may have wanted to have sex with her, but this was not his purpose in approaching her. He was probably just lonely and wanted someone to talk to. What had bothered her so much was the constant interruption of her reading. It is not like she was sitting there looking at the scenery. She was *obviously* engaged with her book. Why would you interrupt someone under those circumstances? It was such a little thing, but Claudia could not help it. It was always the little things that made her lose control.

Timeless Love

Xavier had always loved Sofia. She had been an adorable baby that had become a cute little girl, and who had now blossomed into a beautiful youth on the cusp of womanhood. Xavier had been a witness to all of it. At eighteen, right out of high school, he had taken a job at a plastics factory in the Long Island City area of Queens and settled into a second-floor apartment in the same area. Sofia's family lived right across the street from him in the superintendent's unit on the first floor, that came with an additional patio space which was a bonus that all the other apartments in the complex envied. From this vantage point, Xavier could see Sofia's transformation throughout the years as she spent a lot of time outside and he, in turn, spent countless hours looking outside his kitchen window.

Although the three-year anniversary of her moving in with him was coming up, their romance had begun long before. Of course, it was a forbidden romance. No one could know about their love because it would not be understood. He was, after all, twice her age, and there were many problems that came along with that, not the least of which was the fact that he was a grown man while Sofia was still technically a minor. Apart from being socially unacceptable, it was against the law.

Luckily for Xavier and Sofia, her eighteenth birthday was just around the corner, and they would then be able to celebrate their love in public. Undoubtedly, there would be more than a few furrowed brows and sidelong stares, but that was a small price to pay for being able to show the world that their relationship was just as legitimate as anyone else's. Although Xavier lived under the constant fear of being accused of a crime for being in a relationship with someone who was still legally a child, it had been especially difficult for Sofia.

She had not left Xavier's apartment in the last three years. It was too risky with her family living right across the street. It was true that she never complained and was always in a good mood when Xavier got home from work. They would spend hours talking about their future, followed by nights of incredible love and passion. They were the perfect couple. How could anybody possibly find fault with that? Still, it was better to be prudent. Even though the age of consent in New York was seventeen, waiting until Sofia's eighteenth birthday to return to the outside world would guarantee safety for both as she would be considered a full-fledged adult.

Although the prospect of being able to profess their love to the world was an attractive one, Xavier could not help feeling a sense of dread as well. Sofia had moved in with him on her fifteenth birthday. Legally speaking, he had held a minor captive for three years and could very well spend the rest of his life in prison for sexual assault and kidnapping. The courts would not care that Sofia had been a willing participant. He would be labeled as a child predator and not last long in the world of the living if incarcerated.

On the other hand, all aspects of crime and punishment aside, Sofia would go back out into the world after being under the sole protection and care of Xavier. She would be eager to meet new people and experience new things. She would be seduced by everything life has to offer a beautiful young woman. What is to say she would even want to come back to Xavier after tasting the delicious fruits of freedom?

Xavier thought back to the evening when Sofia's life had become exclusively his. It was her fifteenth birthday and as usual, Xavier was staring longingly at her outside his kitchen window. It was a hot summer morning and Sofia was dressed in denim shorts and a cut-off blouse. Her long, wavy, jet-black hair and her dark eyes complemented her bronze skin beautifully. She had a sweet demeanor about her, which was very endearing and child-like, but contrasted starkly with her body, which was that of a fully developed woman. Xavier could not help but be drawn to this dichotomy and gasped audibly as he tried to balance feelings of ethereal love with carnal lust.

Sofia was clearly excited about the preparations for the day's festivities. The Latino community in Queens took *Quinceañera* celebrations very seriously and would go all out, regardless of socioeconomic status or even budget possibilities. Many families would break the bank and get into debt up to their eyeballs trying to outdo each other as long as their little girl could have a memorable *Quinceañera* celebration. Although a bit outdated for the times, the tradition called for young girls to be introduced into society as young women at age fifteen.

Even though it was not yet noon, and the party would not officially begin until the evening, Sofia was out and about with her mother as they received musicians, caterers and decorators as well as dealing with extended family members and curious neighbors who, with or without official invitations, would make their way to the soiree which promised to last until the early hours of the morning.

It was the weekend, so Xavier did not have to work. He spent the entire day joyfully observing the comings and goings, but when evening arrived and guests started arriving in formal attire, a great melancholy feeling took over his mood. This was a big day for Sofia. As her significant other, he should be there at her side. Who cared what people thought? After all, it was not like he was an old man. He had recently turned thirty. There were plenty of couples with an even bigger age gap between them. Why should he and Sofia be any different? After considering all the possible outcomes of showing up to her party uninvited and claiming amorous rights over Sofia, he decided against it. Xavier loved her too much to put her in any sort of compromising, or even dangerous position. He did have to talk to her, though. That much was certain, so he maintained sentinel duty at his window until he could speak to her privately.

Several hours passed before the opportunity finally presented itself. The door to Sofia's family's apartment remained open all night. Guests would occasionally step out for a breath of fresh air or simply for a respite from the blaring music and crowded apartment. Some of the teenagers would come out to smoke, drink, or make out with each other away from parental supervision. Not that it made any difference. By midnight, most of the adults present were too drunk to notice or even care about such trivialities. It *was* a party after all. A little after two o'clock in the morning, Sofia stepped out onto the street. She looked absolutely stunning in a fitted blue dress and matching gold necklace and earrings. Her face was a bit flushed, but she had on it the overwhelming, fresh happiness that only a fifteen-year-old girl can exude. It was obvious that she was anxious to begin her life with Xavier.

Anxious to not postpone their life together any longer, Xavier called out to her. "Sofia! Sofia!"

Sofia looked across the street, and although it was very dark, she could recognize the voice of her beloved anywhere. "I'm here, baby. I love you. Now we'll never have to be apart again. I love you," she answered as she made her way across the street to Xavier's building.

The sound of screeching tires and the smell of burnt rubber brought Xavier back to the present. He looked out his window, but the street was empty. It was a good distraction from his trip down memory lane, though. Three years had passed since that night and he decided to confront Sofia on her eighteenth birthday to determine what the next step in their relationship would be.

As usual, Sofia greeted him with a kiss full of sweetness that nonetheless portended a night of fiery passion. Hesitant to have such a serious conversation but aware of the need to do so, Xavier gently pushed Sofia away and led her to a nearby chair. "Honey, we need to talk."

"I've heard enough break-up dialogues to know that those words mean trouble," answered Sofia in a joking manner, but showing a hint of concern in her eyes, nevertheless.

"This is serious, love. You know that today is the big day."

"I know. I know. Can't we talk about this later?" she replied, sidling up to him again in a flirtatious manner. Although three years had passed, Sofia looked and acted the same as she had for her *Quinceañera* celebration. Although on the cusp of womanhood, she was still very much a child.

Xavier took a gentle but firm tone with Sofia. "We're talking about it now. Your family needs to know about us. You're an adult now and you need to start behaving like one."

Apparently, gentle but firm did not sit well with Sofia. "So now you want to treat me like an adult? After all this time living exclusively for you. Looking like you want me to look. Saying the things that you want to hear. Doing absolutely everything for you, and never complaining once about always being locked up in this crappy apartment. Now I'm an adult?" She stood up furiously and was gone.

Xavier was certainly not expecting such a reaction from Sofia. After years of sweet submission, she had finally had enough. He was so shocked at her words that he did not even notice her leaving the apartment. It was almost as if she had simply vanished into thin air. Xavier was hurt, but he was not about to give up. A love like theirs could surpass boundaries of societal propriety as well as criminal justice. Were not the best things in life those worth fighting for? He knew what he had to do.

Xavier showered, shaved, put on his Sunday best, and bought some fresh flowers at the corner stand. He marched confidently over to Sofia's parents' apartment, determined to legitimize his relationship with their daughter.

Sofia's mother answered the door. Although barely in her forties, she looked like an old woman. Her hair had gone gray prematurely, and deep wrinkles had formed on her face from so much suffering. She managed a weak smile for Xavier and said, "Are you here for the memorial? How nice of you to come. You know, today would have been her eighteenth birthday."

The sound of hysterical screams from the woman brought neighbors out into the street. Xavier's eyes had bulged out horrifically. He had clutched at his chest in pain with a gnarled hand and fallen dead right at her feet.

THREE YEARS EARLIER

Sofia exited the apartment in a rush of nervous excitement. She had just shared a passionate kiss with Mario. She knew that at seventeen, Mario already had the reputation of being a player in the neighborhood, but she also knew that she would be the woman to tame him. She would have liked to hold that kiss forever, but she knew that an older man like Mario had probably kissed a hundred girls, and she did not want to seem too eager, so she pulled away from him and ran out into the street. Surely, Mario would come out after her. It was just a matter of time.

Suddenly she heard a male voice calling her from across the street. It was quite dark, but she thought she could make out the features of the chubby, balding guy on the second floor that was always staring at her through his window. He always creeped her out with his lecherous face, but this time she was going to give the dirty old pervert a piece of her mind. Mario was her boyfriend now, and the word on the street was that he was in a gang as well. He would put the old man in his place.

Sofia walked out into the street looking straight ahead of her without breaking a stride, so she had no time to react when the car driven by a stoned teenager intending to crash the party plowed right into her. The final sensations Sofia experienced were the sound of screeching tires and the smell of burnt rubber.

The Ultimate Sacrifice

William Covington opened his eyes suddenly and saw the same thing he saw every time he opened his eyes. A question mark about the size of a man's fist was exactly in the center of his field of vision. It was not clearly defined. It looked like what a small child would produce in his earliest attempts at writing, not much more than an illegible scribble, but it *was* a question mark. Of that, William was certain.

He turned his head to the left and the clock read 11.55 p.m. Was it almost noon or almost midnight? William did not know. He had more important things on his mind, so it really did not matter. These days nothing much mattered to William. He turned his face back toward the ceiling and stared at the question mark. The question mark was surrounded by an array of symbols and drawings. These had different meanings depending on how you looked at them. There was a profile of a woman's face that could just as well be a man with a beer belly. There was also a sailboat that could pass for a butcher knife with an unnaturally wide blade, a bit of a stretch, true, but not at all impossible.

Cracks on the ceiling have that special magic about them. They can reshape themselves to suit the spectator's imagination, much in the same manner as clouds in the sky, but William did not have time for such romantic notions as clouds in the sky, or raindrops on roses, or whiskers on kittens. He focused once again on the question mark. It was the only crack on the ceiling that could not be anything else, no matter how many times he tried looking at it differently. It was always a question mark, nothing more, nothing less, or *was* there something more?

A loud clicking next to his left ear brought William back to earth with a slight jump. He turned his head once again and the clock read 11.56 p.m. The sound that he heard was the analog clock switching digits.

"What kind of hotel still uses analog clocks?" he asked the empty room.

The only other sound was that of a rusty old fan slowly panning left and right to circulate the thick, hot air around him.

"The same kind that doesn't even bother installing a fucking air conditioner," he mumbled to himself.

William sat up on his bed and realized that he was drenched in sweat. How could he have possibly been reduced to this? It did not make any sense to him. William's family had immigrated to the United States from England when he was barely ten years old. He had been raised and educated in the best private schools that New England had to offer, and he had all the corresponding degrees to prove it. When he had moved to New York, he was already a well-respected academician with a combination of old and new money that allowed him to live an extremely comfortable life. So, what had happened? What had he done wrong? He was forty-five years old and living in a roach-infested, tenth-rate hotel in Hell's Kitchen. This was the type of place where petty drug dealers conducted their business, where disease-ridden hookers provided cheap thrills for their customers, where an unstable, solitary youth with idle hands could very well begin his emotional and psychological training to become a mass murderer.

William pushed these thoughts out of his mind with a hard slap to his stubbly cheek. It was bad enough he had to share living quarters with these types of individuals. Dwelling upon it would not make it any better. Besides, he did not have much time left. He had to … Had to what? He did not remember. This whirlwind of thoughts made his head feel heavy. He flopped back down into a puddle of his own sweat and stared straight ahead. There it was as always, a crudely-formed question mark holding his stare with its defiant, child-like shape.

He remained in this manner for what seemed like hours, staring intensely at the question mark in front of him, hardly thinking and breathing in long, deep swallows of air in almost perfectly equal intervals. His thoughts drifted back to a faculty party he had attended long ago. He had never really enjoyed these functions, but his position and social status required him to attend them and his performance of brilliant and charming gentleman during such events was truly Oscar-worthy.

At first, he had felt like a total hypocrite and would comment on it during the sporadic conversations he would have with his mother on the telephone. She had moved back to England when he had gone off to college and as the years went by, their communication had dwindled until it was reduced to an occasional call on a birthday or holiday from either party. He did remember one conversation with her very vividly, though. It was after he had attended his first faculty event. Back then he had only been a graduate teaching assistant, but he was already making a name for himself in the world of academia through his work and social graces.

"It's horrible, Mother. I feel like a complete fake!"

"Calm down, dear. You're being overly dramatic."

"I'm really not. These things are just a bunch of arrogant, self-indulgent assholes stroking each other's egos. They might as well just go up to the podium and jack off because really, that's all they're doing."

"For heaven's sake, William! Don't be so vulgar. Is that what you've learned from your time in America?"

"I'm sorry, Mother. It's just so irritating. I can't be like them. I won't be like them."

There had been a deep sigh on the other end of the line and a short pause. Then his mother had simply said, "You can, and you will."

William had been shocked and disappointed at his mother's bleak and cynical response. Being the passionate, twenty-five-year-old that he was at the time, he had tried countering her answer with the beginning of a long-winded oral essay on the importance of human sincerity and the wrongs of succumbing to hypocrisy in social settings. Mrs. Covington apparently had no intention of sitting through this young idealist's proclamation, so she simply cut him off mid-monologue.

"I'm sorry, sweetheart. Your father will be home any minute and I want to make sure that his dinner is served properly this time. A couple of nights ago, he screamed at the maid for adding too much Parmesan cheese to his pasta. He said it was very plebian of her."

William had been annoyed that his mother had interrupted him, but the anecdote about the meal turned his annoyance into a mild sort of rage. Was she not listening to a word he was saying? He decided that he did not want a confrontation, so he simply said, "Be well, Mother. Give my best to Father."

"I will dear, and remember, William, you are still a young man. Life will show you that it is necessary to adapt to the circumstances around you, even if you don't always agree with them."

With these words she had hung up and William listened to

the dial tone for a full ten seconds before slamming the receiver back into its cradle. William told himself that he would never give in to this bullshit, but, of course, he had not only given in to *this* bullshit, but to a vast collection of bullshit throughout the past twenty years. He had groomed himself, unwillingly but quite successfully, into the hypocritical charmer his mother had predicted he would become. Even though she had been dead over a decade now, he would sometimes imagine her looking at him from wherever it is that dead people dwell with a smug smile that said, I told you so.

Another event that now came into his memory had been in honor of a professor who was retiring. He had taught creative writing for fifty years before the administration had decided that a man who would repeat a lesson two or three times in a row due to senility was not much of an asset to the university. Of course, they gave him all the pomp and circumstance that was expected, cried their crocodile tears, and sent him on his way with a gold watch to keep him company in the nursing home that would slowly rob him of his prestige, independence, and eventually his life.

The provost had approached William during the social gathering. She was a stout, matronly woman of about sixty. She had been to all the right places and knew all the right people. She had a graceful manner about her and an unquenchable thirst for gossip. She sidled up to William in what she mistakenly thought was a casual manner. "Good evening, Professor Covington. What a pleasure it is to have you here tonight."

"The pleasure is mine, Provost Richards," he said gallantly. As he bent down to press his cheek against hers, she blew a kiss into the air. William thought sourly that of all the fake social graces imaginable, this had to be one of the worst.

"I see you have decided to go stag tonight, William."

William just smiled politely but did not say a word.

"Where is your... Oh, dear... How shall I say it... Your special friend?"

William could now feel his right temple begin to throb slowly, but he kept his composure. "I believe you mean my girlfriend," William answered, his polite smile struggling to maintain its position.

"Oh, yes, of course... girlfriend," Provost Richards said as she looked around the room. She seemed embarrassed by the word. "What was her name? Sandy? Candy? All these girls have similar names."

William's fake smile now disappeared altogether and his answer came out in a low growl. "Mandy."

"Mandy," he said aloud to the empty hotel room. The name echoed in his mind like a sweet musical note.

The sudden sound of the clock next to him made him jump up violently in the bed and a short gasp escaped his mouth. He looked around and for a few horrifying seconds he did not know where he was. He saw the clock displayed 11.57 p.m. and remembered. This was his existence now. This was his time and his place. The great William Covington was now just another loser sharing dwelling space with a bunch of disgusting rats, both of the human and the four-legged variety. He craned his head upward and heard the tendons in his neck creak. Once again, his sight focused on the question mark on the ceiling. That damned question mark! Always there, always asking but never offering even the slightest hint of an answer. *But what is the question?* William thought.

Suddenly, an irrational fear took over his mind. The question mark was not a question mark at all. It was a hangman's noose, and it was meant for him. It would tighten itself around his throat and squeeze the life out of him as his face turned blue and his eyes bulged out. He ran trembling fingers through his thinning hair and when he looked at his hands, they were covered with blood and hair. He was tearing out his hair and his scalp was gushing fresh blood. This time when the clock changed digits, he screamed out loud and fell out of the bed. He wiped stinging sweat out of his eyes and looked up at the clock from the floor. It read 11.58 p.m. His hands and head were unmarked. There was not even a trace of blood on them. "Get a grip, William. What the hell is the matter with you?" he scolded himself.

He forced himself to stand up on legs that felt like rubber and sat down on the edge of the bed. He took a bottle of water from the top of the night table and drank in greedy, noisy gulps. When he had finished half the bottle, he poured the rest of it over his head and let it run down his face, neck, shoulders, chest and back. The feeling of the cool water on his hot skin was incredible. It was like being under the world's smallest waterfall. It was like soft, beautiful chamber music. It was like… Mandy. Once again, the name entered his mind like heavenly music and his thoughts wandered.

Mandy had been born Raymonda Ganes in some God-forsaken, smaller-than-small town somewhere in New York State. She had once told William the name, but he no longer remembered, and that was just as well. Mandy had always been ashamed of her origins and wanted nothing to do with that part of her life if she could help it. She could not always help it, though. Her name itself was a perfectly clear indication of her background. What parent in his right mind would name a baby girl Raymonda? It practically reeked of trailer trash. Mandy had later explained that her father's egomaniacal nature had led him to make all his children his namesakes. Her three older brothers were named Raymond Brian, Raymond Christopher, and Raymond Johnathan. For him, the logical course of action when choosing a name for his daughter was a variation of his own name, hence Raymonda came into existence.

Mandy had moved to the city right after high school. Her excellent grades and various extracurricular activities had earned her a full scholarship at the university where William taught. Her father had no problem letting her go. He thought the only reason a woman should go to college is to find a husband and he would rather she marry a rich, city guy than a drunk, wife-beating townie like himself. It was one fewer thing to worry about.

William first met Mandy in his Introduction to Literature seminar. This was the first mandatory course for all English majors and mostly consisted of freshman and sophomores with only a few exceptions. According to William's colleagues, teaching this course was beneath him due to his credentials and history at the university, but William did not mind. In fact, he rather enjoyed shaping young minds fresh out of high school.

Mandy was by no means a raving beauty, but she was a pretty girl. She had long, wavy blonde hair and green eyes. Her skin was fair, and she had a nice, harmonious body. What attracted William the most was that she did not have that slutty look that most of the other attractive girls and some of the not-so-attractive girls did. She had a soft sensuality about her eyes, but her eyes did not scream out *do me* as so many others had in his long tenure at the university. William was not naïve, though. He was in his forties and did not equate soft beauty with purity, much less virginity. Mandy had surely had her share of sexual encounters. Girls with her background were generally deflowered early on in life, many times by fathers, uncles, or brothers. It was an awful fact, but a fact, nonetheless.

William's relationship with Mandy seemed to have materialized out of thin air. It began with shy looks during class which rapidly evolved into not-so-shy looks after class. A cup of coffee here, a candlelight dinner there, a weekend at the beach here, two weeks in Florida there. It seemed to escalate at an alarming speed and before they knew it, they were in love.

They lived their romance to the fullest, not caring what people said behind their backs and caring even less when the occasional brave soul said something to their faces. The age difference did not seem to matter to them. Mandy would accompany William to his social events and William would in turn, go out to dance clubs with Mandy and her friends. It was a perfect situation. William taught at a university where there was no such thing as a fraternization policy. They were in seventh heaven with zero problems... but... was that really possible... zero problems? William did not think so, and he was right.

Toward the end of the first semester Mandy was at the university, she started to become a little distant and moody. By this time, they were already living together in William's apartment. One Saturday morning over breakfast, William decided to confront her. "What's wrong, honey?" he asked her.

"Nothing," she answered without looking up from her plate.

William reached over and touched her face. "Come on, baby. You can tell me."

She pulled away from him a bit too brusquely. Then she stood up from the table and walked toward the sink. She faced William and saw his expression of mixed pain and surprise. "I'm sorry, Billy. I just think we should cool it for a while."

William could not believe his ears. How could she possibly be saying these words to him? The ungrateful little bitch! He had taken her in, taught her how to dress and given her the love and affection that her white trash family never had. How dare she?

As if reading his thoughts, Mandy started crying and said, "I'm not some social experiment for you to show off. I know what people say. That sly, inbred cunt from the boondocks came to the big city, spread her legs for the first mature teacher that smiled at her and hit a fucking gold mine in the process. Rags to Riches 101, Professor Covington."

William could still not get over what he was hearing. True, what she said made a lot of sense. He was old enough to be her father, perhaps even old enough to be her father's older brother, but that did not matter to them, did it? "I thought you didn't care what people said," he said stupidly. He could not think of anything better to say.

Clearly exasperated, Mandy threw up her arms and left without saying a word, leaving William alone in the kitchen. With Mandy gone, William did not have a date for that night's social event. He was in incredibly low spirits for the rest of the day, which made Provost Richard's words even more irritating. Oh yes, of course… girlfriend. The words pierced his heart, mind, and soul like little daggers. What he needed was… more water?

William looked up at the bottle of water he was holding above his head. It was empty. Once again, he was startled by the loud click of the clock. It was 11.59 p.m. Had it only been four minutes since he woke up? That seemed impossible, but time had a strange way of manifesting itself when you were alone, especially when you were *all* alone.

William threw the empty bottle across the room and it made a perfect landing inside the wastebasket that would have made his high school basketball coach proud. He stood up, stretched out his limbs and looked around the room. *This really is a shithole*, he thought. The walls were a yellowish white with nasty specks of black that made William think of rotting teeth. The drawn drapes were dark blue with a blanket of dust almost as thick as the drapes themselves. The only furniture was the bed, the night table and what remained of what would probably have been a nice dresser during World War II. The air stank of liquor and cigarettes and he could also smell a combination of feces, urine and semen that made him want to gag. *How could anyone live like this?* he wondered, but, of course, *he* was here. William Covington, Ph.D., who played tennis on the weekends and belonged to a wine club was in this very room. Why?

William stood very still and evaluated his current situation. He did not remember moving into this hotel. In fact, he did not even remember checking in. He thought about this for a moment and realized that he could not remember what his last meal had been or whom his last conversation had been with. He could not remember any of these things. His most recent memories always came back to this room, this dank, dirty, disgusting prison of a room. How did he come to be here in the first place?

He was about to follow this train of when the clock alarm went off breaking his concentration. It was a loud, piercingly strident sound that made his ears hurt. He covered his ears with his hands and looked at the clock. It read 12.00 a.m. and that was when everything started to change. The room began to shimmer as if it were shaking, and objects began materializing before his very eyes. Slowly, clothing, magazines, and food started appearing scattered around the room. The room was obviously still a dump, but at least now, it looked lived-in. He heard a voice and turned toward the bed. A woman was lying on her back with a cheap, faux leather miniskirt pulled above her waist. She was smoking a cigarette and without removing it from her mouth, turned to William and asked, "Are you done?"

The question confused William and just as he was about to attempt an answer, he heard a high-pitched man's voice coming from behind him. "Yeah, I'm done, you stupid whore, but I'm not happy. I can tell you that."

William turned around and saw a small, nerdy-looking man putting on his pants. He was bald, skinny, and had beady little eyes covered by large, horn-rimmed glasses. William guessed he was an accountant, or perhaps a banker. He turned back to the woman on the bed, who was pulling down her skirt to cover herself. She could not be any older than twenty-five, but her haggard appearance and sunken eyes made her look more like fifty. She chuckled briefly, took a couple of puffs from her cigarette, put it out on the ashtray on the night table, and then said in a raspy, smoker's voice, "Who is?"

The little man looked mildly annoyed as he continued getting dressed. "Ramon said you would be worth my money."

"Ramon says that about all his girls. It's called speculation. You should know that, being a Wall Street guy and all."

William had been wrong. The little man with the beady eyes was a stockbroker. Well, close enough.

"Besides," the woman continued, "a man as loaded as you should go uptown and get yourself some classy pussy, and when I say loaded, I mean your wallet, 'cause otherwise..." At this point she trailed off into a whispery bout of giggles.

It did not take a genius to figure out what was happening here. This woman was either drunk or stoned, probably both. This was a business transaction gone sour. The client had paid for a service and was not satisfied with what he had received. No matter how sordid a business prostitution was, William did not think it a wise course of action to make fun of your clients, no matter how small they were, pun most definitely intended.

As if he were listening to William's thoughts, the bald man said, "You think you can make fun of me just because I'm small?"

This was the wrong choice of words for the occasion. The young woman's giggles quickly escalated into a loud, loathsome bray of vulgar laughter. She contained herself between cackles just long enough to say, "Well, you certainly are small!"

William felt a mounting horror swell up inside him. This was not going to turn out well. In fact, this was going to turn out very badly, very badly indeed. In response to William's premonition, the man dashed across the room and jumped on top of the woman on the bed. He put his arms out as if to punch her, but she grabbed hold of his scrawny elbows and he looked like an angry toddler protesting that it was too early to go to sleep. Under any other circumstances, this scene would have been extremely comical, worthy of being acted out by the likes of Charlie Chaplin or Mr. Bean, but the circumstances were far from humorous.

Unfortunately, the woman did not seem to understand this. The sight of this weak, wimpy man on top of her was just too hilarious. It made her laugh even harder and shake all over. She loosened her grip on his right elbow. First mistake. His right fist connected with her right breast. The laughter stopped immediately and was replaced by a cry of pain. She closed both her hands over her wounded breast. Second mistake. Now both the man's hands were free. He connected his left fist with her abdomen and the air was taken out of her. As she gasped, he interlocked the fingers of both his hands together as if offering a prayer and brought them down hard on her throat, damaging her trachea. Her eyes bulged out and she started turning blue.

He finally got off her and walked toward the other side of

the room. William watched in terror as the man picked up a tennis racket and walked back to the gasping woman. He looked down at her, producing a sinister smile and said, "That'll teach you to make fun of me you filthy, fucking cunt." He raised the tennis racket over his head and brought it down repeatedly on the woman's head, chest, and legs.

William tried to scream, but nothing came out of his mouth. He felt totally incapable of movement. He just watched the tennis racket moving up and down. The woman was convulsing, and he could see the blood splatter on the small man's face, hands, and chest. William closed his eyes and continued hearing wood and wire breaking bone and the squelching sound of blood and torn muscle. He remained that way for a long time.

When he finally opened his eyes, the man was gone, and the woman was lying still. William felt completely nauseous. As soon as he found the willpower to move, he would get out of here. He had been in this room long enough. When he finally felt he could move, he turned toward the door and was preparing to leave when something caught his eye. The bald, little man who worked on Wall Street had thrown the tennis racket into the wastebasket. William thought this a bit unusual considering the gruesome murder that had just taken place, but who knew the workings of the human mind, especially when it came to crimes of passion.

The handle was sticking out and William could see that there was something engraved in the wood. This is ridiculous. Who cares what it says? Just leave. But something inside him would not let him leave until he saw what was written on the damned racket. He knew that as surely as he knew that the crack on the ceiling was a question mark, always a question mark and never anything else. He walked toward the wastebasket and bent down to see what it read on the handle of the racket. He did not want to touch it, but he needed to know what it read. At first, he could not accept what he was seeing, but when he read it again several times, there was no doubt in his mind. The dead prostitute on the bed was Mandy. The inscription on the handle read:

WILLIAM COVINGTON AND MANDY GANES
  DOUBLES TOURNAMENT CHAMPIONS
  DRAGON'S CLUB
  NEW YORK, 2000

William looked up at the wall above the wastebasket. There was a calendar displaying July 2005. The clock on the night table still read 12.00 a.m. While William was desperately trying to make sense of all this information, he heard a sudden sound behind him. Mandy's mangled corpse was walking toward him with open arms. He did not know if she meant to hug him or strangle him, but neither prospect seemed particularly attractive to him. He tried to scream but once again, nothing came out.

She was moaning through a mouthful of broken teeth. "Why, Billy? Why, Billy? Why, Billy?" An image of the crack on the ceiling that was always a question mark and never anything else came to William's mind and finally, he remembered everything.

A couple of weeks after the conversation he and Mandy had had over breakfast, if you could call that a conversation, he had convinced her that the two of them should take a trip together after the semester was over. It would do them good to get away from everybody and concentrate on their relationship. William had a small boat on City Island. It was the only reason he ever ventured into the Bronx. The only other reasons to go to that horrible borough was to either watch a game at Yankee Stadium if you were a baseball fan or visit the Bronx Zoo if you were an animal lover. Luckily, William was neither.

They chose a date and it coincided with the six-month anniversary of their first date. What could be more perfect? A few days before the departure, the boat's mechanic called and said that William's personal assistant had informed him that William planned to go from City Island to Montauk Point with his girlfriend and no crew. William confirmed that this was true. He had been on the boat enough times to handle the trip by himself. He did not allow himself to be dissuaded despite the mechanic's insistence that they should have an experienced person on board with them. William was planning to ask Mandy to marry him, and it would simply not be as romantic with someone else accompanying them. Besides, the mechanic had been nagging like his mother and William was a grown man. He knew what he was doing.

Unfortunately, it turned out that William did *not* know what he was doing. Three hours after departing from the dock at City Island, he and Mandy were sitting on an inflatable lifeboat in the middle of the water. William had no idea where they were. He only knew that his boat was gone along with all the supplies, including the oars for the lifeboat. It would probably be filed away as mechanical failure, but William knew damn well that it should be filed away as arrogant stupidity. He could see his mother's smug smile. *I told you so.*

Mandy did not say a single word to him during their time on the lifeboat. She simply scowled at him with pouty lips that made her look ten years younger than she was. This made William uncomfortable for many reasons. They were on the boat for nearly three days before the Coast Guard finally found them. Lack of food and fresh water, and the effects of sunstroke had them veering closer and closer to death. On the eve of the day they were found, William had a vision too vivid to be a hallucination, although hallucinations under these extreme circumstances were quite common. Mandy was lost in delirious sleep and William was just beginning to doze off when he suddenly saw his mother standing beside him. She was sort of floating above the water, but she seemed as secure in her stance as if she were standing firmly on dry land.

"Hello, Mother. What are you doing here?" he asked groggily.

"I'm here because you need to make a choice," she answered sternly. William rubbed his eyes expecting the image of his mother to disappear, but it remained exactly where it was.

"Come now, William. There isn't much time left," she pressed on.

"Mother, I'm dying," he said weakly.

"All the more reason to decide quickly, dear."

"Decide? Decide what?"

"Who is coming with me and who is staying here."

"Are you saying that Mandy and I are already dead?

"Not quite yet, but time is running out and if you don't decide soon, I will have to take both of you with me."

William finally understood what his mother was telling him. It was up to him to decide who lived and who died. *He* was in control. *He* had the final say. *He* had the power. Of course, he did not want the power. Why should anyone have to make such a decision? It was not fair. He turned to say just that to his mother, or at least the apparition posing as his mother, but she started to fade away. "Please hurry, William. Time is almost up," she said in a pleading tone.

He looked over at Mandy, his young, beautiful Mandy. He

genuinely loved her. He had not thought he would be able to love so intensely after his first marriage failed, but he had been wrong. Mandy had made everything new and fresh and lovely again. He said to the shimmering shape of his mother, "Take me, mother. I want to go with you."

His mother's voice answered in a nearly inaudible whisper and he thought he heard a touch of sadness in it. "We can only go part of the way together. You need to know that, William." And she was gone.

William took one last look at Mandy and then closed his eyes. He had made the right choice. He had already lived half of his life. Mandy had her whole life ahead of her. He had made the ultimate sacrifice for love.

The next morning the Coast Guard found the lifeboat. Mandy was severely dehydrated, but still had a weak pulse. William was pronounced dead on the spot. It was determined that he had died in his sleep the night before.

William's funeral was a grand event full of mourning faculty and students alike. The eulogy brought tears to many eyes and the attendees treated Mandy very much like the grieving widow. They may not have approved of the relationship, but it was what William would have wanted and at least for today, they would honor his wishes.

Mandy never recovered from William's death. She started smoking, drinking, and doing drugs. Her grades suffered noticeably and when she lost her scholarship, she decided to drop out of school and pursue other interests instead. There was no way in hell she was going back home, so she took waitressing and bartending gigs here and there, but it was not enough to support her addiction. In less than two years' time, she was a strung-out, heroin-addicted hooker working the dirty back alleys of Hell's Kitchen.

These are the consequences of my decision, William thought as the bloody pulp that was once Mandy Ganes approached him wailing, "Why, Billy? Why, Billy? Why, Billy?"

He tried to tell himself that he had done it for love, but he knew it was not true, not really. He had done it out of cowardice. He did not want to be the one who mourned a loved one. He did not want to go through the pain and heartache of losing his girlfriend. He did not want to pick up the pieces of his shattered life, and desperately try to go on with no real reason to live. The ultimate sacrifice, indeed. He had been a coward and he would have to pay dearly for it. This was his own, personal hell. His mother had told him that he could only accompany her part of the way, and she had been right, *again.* William did not know where his mother was, but he was in hell, condemned to forever living the final moments of Mandy's pain and suffering in five infernally long minutes. He would wake up and live the same horrible experience over and over again for all eternity. It would begin at 11.55 p.m. with him unaware of what was to come and end at midnight with his decaying girlfriend walking toward him with her blank, dead eyes asking, "Why, Billy? Why, Billy? Why, Billy?"

Waiting Room

The sterile room was barely big enough for the four prisoners. They were all dressed in white from head to toe: white skullcaps on their recently shaven heads, white sweatshirts, white sweatpants, white socks, and white canvas shoes. The oppressive walls surrounding them were also white, the benches they sat on, even the cuffs that bound their hands and feet were a metallic white attached to a cold, white tile floor. Everything around them looked impossibly new and clean. What kind of prison was this anyway? There were no bars or windows anywhere. There did not seem to be any doors either... except that did not make any sense. How did they enter the room in the first place? Which was the way out? It seemed like they had been there forever, and nobody was telling them anything.

The first one to break the silence was a young man in his early twenties. He had the build of a football player and as he spoke, displayed two rows of beautifully straight teeth. "Man, this is some bullshit. How long are they going to keep us here? I'm an American. I have rights."

A derisive snort was heard in answer to the young man's comments. The respondent was a short, frail-looking elderly man with deep creases lining his entire face and eyes that expressed deep sorrow.

Irritated by the retort, the young man addressed him menacingly, "You have something to say, old man?"

The old man got up so quickly and unexpectedly that the

sound of the chains holding him down startled everyone in the room, but since his aggressor flinched violently back, inadvertently letting out a high-pitched, effeminate scream, the other two prisoners roared in laughter. Embarrassed at losing face so easily, the young man muttered sulkily under his breath, "Fuck all of you."

"Calm down, killer. We don't want to have to sick Gramps on you again." Although fodder for more potential humor, the phrase was delivered in such a dispassionate monotone, that nobody laughed. The speaker looked like a porcelain doll. Her beautiful face looked like it belonged in a Victorian Christmas catalog, but the voice was straight out of an episode of Daria on MTV. She could not have been more than thirteen years old, but her expression was that of a world-weary woman.

The only prisoner that had not made a sound remained silent. He was one of those people of indeterminate age and background. His features could possibly be Asian, Latino, Native American or a combination of the three. He could also be either thirty, fifty or anywhere in between.

Suddenly, the sound of a door opening was heard, and everyone turned to look at the direction of the noise. A gender-neutral voice spoke loudly, "Prisoner seven-six-zero-two-two-one." They all looked around in confusion as there did not seem to be any identifying numbers on any of them. They were also shocked to see a door in the corner that none of them had noticed before. The voice repeated, "Prisoner seven-six-zero-two-two-six." The chains on the silent prisoner were suddenly loosened.

"Guess that's you, lover," said the young girl in the same adult tone, jarring in someone who was technically still a child.

The prisoner stood up, quickly looked around the room, and vanished into the doorway without a sound, the door vanishing right behind him as well. He had not said a single word in the entire time he had been in the white room.

"Freaky!" said the young girl, this time betraying her age with an expression of child-like wonder.

The remaining men looked at each other in adult solidarity, their recent quarrel already long forgotten.

The old man then turned to the girl. "Why are you here, young lady?" he said in a strong Eastern European accent but using perfectly fluent English.

"I don't know. Why are you here?" she asked a bit defensively.

The old man ignored the question and continued "What is the last thing you remember?"

The girl looked to the young man for support and he gave her a reassuring look as if to say *Go ahead. Maybe we can figure this out together.*

The girl resumed her previous adult tone and began, "Well, I guess we'll never see each other again after today, so why not? I had just finished servicing a client when I got a call from Oscar…"

"Wait!" interrupted the young man. "Servicing a client? You're just a kid. Don't tell me you're a…"

"OK. I won't tell you. Now, may I continue with my story?" she replied with a defiant look.

The young man was stunned into silence. The old man's expression did not change at all.

The girl continued. "I got a call from Oscar. He books all my appointments and makes sure all my needs are taken care of." She paused for a moment and blushed visibly. "Oscar loves me." She looked up quickly to see if either of her listeners would challenge the statement. Convinced that they had no intention of doing so, she went on. "He had planned a romantic dinner for the two of us, which was perfect because I had some exciting news. You see… I'm pregnant. Oscar and I are going to have a baby."

The young man could not hold back. "Oh, God," he muttered in despair.

The old man said nothing, but two huge tears rolled down his cheeks.

"No! No! It's not like that," the girl insisted, all her former womanly confidence now gone. "Oscar is not like all the other men I've been with. He really loves me. We're going to be a family. We're going to start a brand-new life together far away from here and…"

"Prisoner seven-one-zero-eight-two-zero."

The girl was now crying like the young child she was. "We're going to raise the baby together, and we're going to be so happy, and…"

"Prisoner seven-one-zero-eight-two-zero."

Her chains were loosened, and she vanished through the same unexpected doorway the first prisoner had, her sobs echoing loudly through the white room.

"Where do you think they're being taken?" asked the young man nervously.

"I have no idea, but I get the feeling that we will find out very soon," answered the old man serenely. "What's the last thing you remember, son?"

"Who cares, Pops? What difference does it make?" he answered in an almost hysterical tone.

"Young man, knowledge is power. We don't know why we're here or what lies beyond that door, but we sure as hell better learn something about our situation fast if we want to have any chance of facing whatever it is we're up against."

"Oh, yeah? And how do you propose we do that?"

"The four of us must have something in common. It's not a coincidence that we were all placed in the same room. We don't remember how we got here, but if we can tap into our last memory before today, maybe we can find a common thread that can help us understand what's happening. Come on. Please. Try to think back. What is the last thing you remember before being locked in a room with three total strangers?"

The young man took a deep breath and let out a long painful sigh. "I had an argument with my grandmother. A pretty nasty one," he said with a look of embarrassment.

"Go on," replied the old man with perfect ease.

"Well, you know..." stammered the young man. "In my community... it's not accepted... to be.... you know... different."

The old man looked at him attentively and motioned for him to continue.

"There was a video of me and... a friend... posted online. My grandmother found out and she went ballistic. She said I was a disgrace to the family and that I was no longer her grandson. It got pretty ugly."

"Young man," the elderly prisoner began, understanding the situation perfectly well, but feeling the need to confirm it nonetheless. "Are you saying that your grandmother disapproved of your being..."

"Prisoner three-nine–one–one-one-zero."

As with the previous inmates, the restraints were loosened on the young man and with a terrified look in his eyes, he exited through the same doorway as the others had before him as the commanding voice repeated, "Prisoner three-nine-one-one-one-zero."

The old man was now left completely alone. His last memory before being in the white room was still very vivid in his mind. He was surrounded by his loved ones. Everyone he cared about was by his side. There were a few tears, but they were all there to support his decision. They knew that the pain had gotten unbearable for him. It was really the most humane thing to do. After a lifetime of toiling to provide for his family, he deserved some dignity at the end. Just as he was remembering the show of love and support from his family, his memories were interrupted.

"Prisoner three-nine-zero-eight-one-eight," the familiar voice boomed as the doorway appeared once again.

Resigned to his fate, whatever it might be, the old man waited for his chains to be loosened as the voice repeated, "Prisoner three-nine-zero-eight-one-eight."

The old man glanced back at the room one last time and what he saw shocked him. As he was leaving, four new prisoners were entering the white room, except, it was not four new people. It was the same four people who had been in the room just moments ago, himself included. Before he even had time to think, the doorway closed and then there was only darkness.

Not too far from the white room were two uniformed officers of androgynous appearance, dressed completely in black, busily entering information into what appeared to be the mainframe of an enormous central command area.

Officer 1: Read the information back to me before we officially confirm sentence.

Officer 2: Prisoner: 760221 – Mode: Single gunshot to the head, Reason: Infected his pregnant wife with venereal disease after extramarital encounter on business trip – Sentence: Life.

Officer 1: Life sentence confirmed. Next.

Officer 2: Prisoner: 710820 – Mode: Slashing of both wrists in bathtub – Reason: Sentimental partner did not accept responsibility for her pregnancy and left her to fend for herself – Sentence – Life.

Officer 1: Life sentence confirmed. Next.

Officer 2: Prisoner: 391110 – Mode: Jumping out a ten-story window – Reason: Embarrassed at the public discovery of his sexuality and subsequent withdrawal of affection from his grandmother – Sentence – Life.

Officer 1: Life sentence confirmed. Next.

Officer 2: Prisoner: 390818 – Mode: Medically assisted toxic chemical mix ingestion – Reason: Physical pain considered unbearable and financial and emotional strain on family deemed unnecessary – Sentence: Life.

Officer 1: Life sentence confirmed. That is the last one for this group.

Officer 2: We seem to be getting more and more of these cases lately. Do suicides always result in life sentences?

Officer 1: Always.

Officer 2: What is the point then? They get a chance at life again and end up killing themselves over and over again. It is an endless cycle. It does not make sense.

Officer 1: It is not our place to decide what makes or does not make sense. It is our job to process the sentences. Next group.

Officer 2: Current occupants of waiting room. Prisoner…"

Wicked Waters

Donovan Blake looked out at the lake in front of him. It was eerily placid for this time of year. The water was almost motionless, except for a few ripples that made sporadic appearances. He fidgeted uneasily in his rocker and felt something remarkably close to fear for a moment, but it quickly subsided back into an inexplicable sense of uneasiness. Donovan had been experiencing this sensation for the past few days, and it always took hold of him when he sat on the balcony of his cabin overlooking the lake.

"Is it time yet, Daddy?" a small, frightened voice asked from behind him.

Donavan turned around and faced his eight-year-old son. The boy looked up at his father with huge, wondering eyes. Donovan turned his gaze once again toward the lake and answered in a low voice. "Not quite yet, Donny. Not quite yet."

Donovan and his son had moved to Lakeside Gardens six months earlier. It was a small, housing complex about two hours away from the city. There were about twenty-five cabins that shared a beautiful, verdant landscape, a small, but extremely well-stocked general store, and of course, the lake. After a lifetime of the hustle and bustle of Manhattan, it was the perfect change for Donovan and Donny, especially after the untimely death of Susan, Donovan's wife, and Donny's mother.

Donovan had met Susan ten years earlier. They were both already well into their forties, and their union simply seemed like the right thing to do. Theirs was no great love story, no epic romance, simply two mature adults who found each other at the right time in their lives. With the years together, Donovan and Susan had grown fonder of each other, but up until the very end, Donovan had never fallen in love with his wife, and always supposed that she had felt the same about him.

That was why Susan's death came as such a great shock to Donovan. The morning after Donovan confessed to his wife that he was in love with a younger woman, Susan was found dead in their apartment. She had overdosed on sleeping pills. Donovan never quite understood why his wife's reaction had been so drastic. Granted, he was not expecting her to congratulate him. He supposed that at least her woman's pride would suffer. But to take her own life? That seemed more than extreme, considering the relationship they had always had.

The younger woman in question, upon hearing about her lover's wife's suicide, decided that she would do without the inconvenience of any melodrama that could arise from her widowed lover's guilty conscience. She broke off the relationship with Donovan immediately. The reason: she had fallen in love with a younger man.

Donovan was now a man in his mid-fifties. He had enjoyed a moderately successful career as a commercial artist for the past thirty years. He had the freedom to work from home, so considering the recent events, he decided to pack up and move to Lakeside Gardens.

The first few weeks after Susan's death had been horrible for both father and son. Donny cried constantly for his mother, and Donovan could find no words to console his son. The situation reached its climax about a week before the move to Lakeside Gardens. It was early evening and Donovan was watching a boxing match on television. Donny had started crying about a half hour earlier and was already reaching hysterics. "I want my mommy!" Donny bawled.

"Come on, son. Not again. OK?"

Donny ignored his father completely. "I want my mommy! Where's my mommy?"

"Settle down, son. We can't go on like this. We've already talked about this. Now go wash your face and get ready for bed."

Donny walked in front of the television set, blocking his father's view of the fight, and stared at Donovan. "Mommy!" he yelled defiantly.

In the background, the two boxers were pummeling each other mercilessly. The fight had gone into extra rounds, and the men looked more like lifeless pulps than human beings. Their punches were wild, lacking any visible technique. They had pushed themselves and each other to the point of total exhaustion.

"Don't do this now, Donny. It's a very bad idea," Donovan warned his son.

He was now beginning to lose focus on what was going on in the fight, but at the same time, the sounds of the severe blows seemed to intensify inside his head. The sound of forceful impact on wet flesh made his head expand painfully, and he felt sick to his stomach.

Donny saw that he was losing his father's attention. He stepped right up to him and placed his small hands on Donovan's temples until they were nose to nose. "Mommy! Mommy! Mommy!" he yelled, and then let out such a high-pitched shriek that Donovan felt fresh, hot pain in his ears.

At that moment, the bell rang, and the fight was over on television. Both boxers collapsed on the canvas, and neither one of them appeared to have plans of getting up any time soon.

Donovan jumped up from the armchair and hit Donny with a vicious, backhand slap. Donny flew back and crashed into the television set. The impact made the channel jump over to a children's program where multicolored puppets were singing and dancing.

"Shut the fuck up, you disgusting little maggot!" Donovan roared at his son. "Your mother had a prescription cocktail for breakfast and she's not coming back, so just... deal with it!"

Donny stared at his father in disbelief. Donovan had never laid a finger on him. Without a word, a sound, or even a tear. Donny picked himself up, and scurried to his room, closing the door quickly behind him.

Horrified at what he had just done, Donovan quickly went over to his son's bedroom, but Donny had locked the door. Donovan apologized repeatedly, and pleaded with his son to be let in, but it was to no avail. Donovan decided that his son was in shock, and that trying to reason with him at this time would be futile, so he went to his own bedroom, perhaps not the best parenting decision, but his head was throbbing, and he had no energy to deal with the situation at this precise moment.

The next morning, when Donovan woke up, his headache was completely gone. He decided that he would have a long talk with Donny, but first, he would fix himself a hot cup of coffee. When he entered the kitchen, Donny was already at the table eating cereal. His little legs dangled from the chair as he hummed a little song to himself. Donovan thought he recognized the tune from one of the cartoons that Donny liked to watch.

"Hi, Daddy," Donny said cheerfully through a mouthful of brightly colored oats. A nasty bruise had already formed on his cheek.

Ordinarily, Donovan would have scolded his son for his lack

of decorum but was too taken aback by his son's chipper greeting to say anything.

"Can I watch the Teenage Mutant Ninja Turtles?"

"In a minute, son," Donovan answered. "First we need to talk about last night."

Donny finished his last spoonful of cereal and wiped his mouth with his pajama sleeve. "It's OK, Daddy. I know that Mommy is in heaven, and that the angels are taking care of her, and that you and I should be happy because Mommy is happy now too."

"That's right, Donny..." Donovan began cautiously, "and Mommy..."

"And Mommy will always be with us because she will always love us and wants us to be happy too," Donny interrupted. "Right, Daddy?"

"Right," Donovan answered in amazement.

"Can I watch my cartoon now?"

Donovan nodded, and with that, Donny ran into the den, and turned on his program.

"Go Donatello! Turtle Power!" he yelled in delight. Donatello was his favorite turtle because his brothers called him Donny.

Donovan was left alone in the kitchen trying to figure out what had just happened. He had never heard his son speak with such eloquence, and with such self-assurance. Could he really be that mature regarding the death of his mother? Deep inside, Donovan did not think so. However, the idea of just letting things settle on their own was just too tempting. He had dreaded having another long, painful conversation with his son, but now it seemed unnecessary. Was this just him being a cowardly father? Donovan *struggled* with the decision for about thirty seconds, and conveniently decided to leave things alone for now... or possibly forever.

Susan was never a topic of discussion again. In fact, her name was never mentioned again in the Blake household. It was as if though she had never even existed. Donovan noticed, not without a considerable sense of uneasiness, that his son had packed up all his mother's belongings into boxes, which had been labeled GARBAGE in his awkward child's handwriting. All of Susan's pictures were gone too. Donovan did not know whether Donny had kept them, or thrown them away, but he did not dare ask.

Donovan was fully aware that his passiveness to his son's actions was not only highly irresponsible, but quite pathetic. After all, he was not only the adult in the household, but the paternal figure as well. It was his duty to look after the physical and emotional welfare of his child. There seemed to be nothing wrong with his body, but his state of mind could not possibly be healthy. No eight-year-old boy, regardless of his level of maturity, gets over the death of his mother overnight. Donovan knew all of this, and hated himself for it, but cowardice had once again taken over, and he had neither the energy nor the desire to stir up a bubbling pot of emotions that he felt incapable of dealing with. So, he simply took the easy path, and decided that everything would work itself out.

A week later, Donovan and Donny were living in Lakeside Gardens. Donovan had set up a home office, and his son had the entire summer to adapt before school started in the fall.

Donny fell in love with Lakeside Gardens from day one. There was plenty of space to run and play all day. He would often come home completely exhausted and go straight to bed without a word of protest, only to get up early the next day, and repeat the routine all over again. This left Donovan with an ideal work environment in the cabin. It was quiet, peaceful, and he did not have to worry about a babysitter. Lakeside Gardens seemed to be a very wholesome community. Most of its residents were retirees. There were a few freelancers like himself, and during the summer there were a few visiting relatives and friends. There had been no reported crimes since its establishment in the early nineties. The most *shocking* event had been that one time a couple of teenagers were caught in the woods getting hot and heavy, but it never really amounted to anything because they were not permanent residents of the community and had just been visiting relatives during the summer.

Many would object to Donovan Blake's hands-off parenting style, but Donny seemed healthy and happy, and the neighbors never once complained about him. Most of all, Donovan was comfortable. He pushed all his feelings of fatherly guilt to the back of his mind, and enjoyed his new, stress-free life.

Donny loved to go to the lake. He liked watching the ducks and had become quite the expert at skipping stones on the water. One day, during one of his outings, Donny was trying to feed the ducks. He was throwing crushed crackers into the water, but the ducks were too far away, and seemed to be ignoring both him, and their potential meal. He started clapping wildly, but the ducks started swimming further away from him.

"You're scaring them," a voice said from behind.

Donny was momentarily startled, but relaxed when he saw a little boy, perhaps a couple of years older than him, standing on the rocks. "I'm just trying to feed them," Donny answered, blushing a little.

The boy waved his hand as if to say that Donny had nothing to be ashamed of. "Your wild clapping makes them think you're angry at them. You need to show them that you're their friend. Do what I do."

The boy started clapping rhythmically, not too quickly, but not too slowly either. Donny attempted to follow the boy's lead but was a bit clumsy.

"No," the boy corrected him. "Listen to the beat. Like this."

He continued his organized clapping and Donny joined in. It took him a while to sync up with his clapping partner, but he finally achieved it.

"There you go!" the boy cheered. "Now keep it up."

After a couple of minutes, the ducks seemed to be attracted to the sound, and found their way to the two boys, and their supply of crackers. The boys laughed and made quacking sounds as the ducks enjoyed their unexpected feast.

"I'm Jacob," the older boy said with a smile.

"I'm Donny," Donny smiled back.

"I just know we're going to be great friends," Jacob said, a bit overdramatically.

"Yeah," said Donny distractedly as he laughed and imitated the movement of the ducks.

Sunday morning came, and Donovan decided that he would take his son to church. This was not something he did often, but he figured if he was aiming for a new start, he might as well make religion a part of his life. Very much like his marriage to Susan, he felt no compulsion or desire to go to church. He simply thought it the appropriate course of action to take. Besides, he had not been the best father lately, and this seemed like a good place to start.

Donny had been an extremely cooperative child since that night that Donovan had hit him before moving to Lakeside Gardens, but now his reluctance to comply was more than obvious.

"But we never go to church!" he exclaimed.

"All the more reason to start," Donovan answered.

"But Jacob is going to teach me how to fish today!" Donny pleaded.

"Who's Jacob?" Donovan asked.

"He's my new friend."

Donovan took a moment to think. He had not seen any other children Donny's age around the complex. Could it possibly be an adult? Donovan did not like that idea. It had the potential of being a creepy situation that he really did not want to deal with.

"Is he a grown-up?" Donovan asked sternly.

"No. He's a boy, but he's much older than me. He's ten," Donny explained.

Donovan was relieved. Still. It would be good to know who this Jacob was. He could be one of the resident's grandsons.

"Well, you and Jacob can fish tomorrow."

"But Daddy!" Donny intoned with a pitch slightly higher than Donovan was comfortable with.

Donovan considered his options quickly. He could be firm with his son and force him to go to church. Of course, this would probably mean pouting, tears, and eventually hysteria on Donny's part. On the other hand, he could save himself a world of grief, and just let Donny have his way. It was an obvious lack of authority on his part as a father. He was also setting a horrible example for his son, but it was painless, so he once again opted for the latter.

"OK, fine, but I want you to bring Jacob back with you for lunch."

"Thanks, Daddy!" Donny rushed over and wrapped his arms around his father. "Bye bye," he said cheerfully and ran out of the house.

Jacob never made it to lunch and Donovan never made to church. In fact, he would never set foot in a church again for the rest of his life. Donny ran all the way to the meeting point with Jacob. When he got there, he was almost out of breath, and more than a little disappointed to see that Jacob was accompanied by a girl.

"Who's she?" Donny asked, foregoing all pleasantries.

"She's my sister. Her name is Laura."

"Hi," Laura said, and gave Donny a smile that made him blush from head to toe.

"Hi," Donny answered, trying unsuccessfully to appear nonchalant. He generally did not like girls, but the golden-haired beauty before him made him feel tingly all over. "I'm Donny."

"I know who you are, Donny," she said and gave him another smile that made Donny fall instantly in love.

Jacob observed this exchange and grimaced. "OK, lovebirds. We've got some fishing to do."

The three children laughed and went off to the rockiest part of the lake. Jacob, being the oldest, and presumably the wisest, took the lead. He explained that it was easier to fish where there were more rocks because the fish were likely to get trapped between rocks and have less room and time to escape after being captured. Donny asked if it was dangerous, but Laura explained that it consisted of being careful, and not fishing where the rocks were too close to each other.

Jacob put up his hand to silence the other children. He went to a rock with jagged edges and perched himself on top of it like a bird of prey. "I'm ready," he said.

"We need to get supplies first," Donny protested. "Where are the rods and the lines. What are we going to use for bait?"

"We have no use for those trifles, Donovan," Jacob answered in a flat tone.

"Donovan is my father. Everyone calls me Donny," Donny corrected his friend.

Jacob answered in a child's voice, but his tone was unmistakably that of an adult. "We all become one with our father eventually."

With these words, he suddenly dropped on all fours, and submerged his head completely underwater.

A little gasp escaped Donny. Laura quickly took his hand and squeezed gently. "Don't worry, Donny. Jacob knows what he's doing."

Donny watched in amazement as Jacob's head remained underwater for a full five minutes. He then suddenly emerged with a trout trapped between his teeth. He looked at Donny with wild eyes for a moment, and then started to shred the helpless animal apart with deliberate slowness. He wanted every unnerving, squelching sound of his victim's demise to be clearly audible for Donny. He then opened his mouth wide, revealing a disgusting array of mangled fish parts, and issued a spine-tingling guttural laugh.

"Stop it, Jacob! You're frightening him!" Laura scolded her brother. She then took Donny's face in her hands and looked at him with affection. "Don't pay attention to him, Donny. He just likes to show off. We're not all like him."

Laura's warm gaze comforted Donny slightly, but not enough to want to remain at the lake. "I have to go home," he said and ran all the way back to his cabin without looking back. Laura turned to Jacob and gave him a reproachful look, but he simply shrugged his shoulders with indifference.

For the next week, Donny absolutely refused to set foot

outside of the cabin. Donovan kept asking him what was wrong, but Donny simply told him that he wanted to watch cartoons and play with his toys at home. Donovan did not press him. His son was quiet and did not disturb his work. It had probably been a silly argument with this Jacob character, whom he had never gotten a chance to meet. He was sure that Donny would eventually feel the urge to play outdoors, and he was right.

After the second full week of staying in, Donny was dying of boredom. He convinced himself that the whole scary fish incident had been a product of his overactive imagination. He told his father that he was going to play outside, and Donovan felt sure that he had made the right decision by not pressing his son. *Children are just moody,* he told himself and felt content with this flimsy explanation.

Donny went directly to where he had last seen Jacob and Laura. He felt uneasy because the place brought back memories of what he had *imagined*, and, because he was not sure how his friends would react at seeing him again.

"Hello, Donovan," Jacob's voice said from behind him.

"I told you my name is Donny," Donny said with a not-quite-steady voice.

"I knew you would return, Donovan," Jacob said, ignoring the remark.

"Welcome back, Donny," Laura said as she appeared on the other side of him. She then gave Donny a hug and kiss that made the blood run to his cheeks.

"I want you to meet our sister, Janie..." Jacob pointed toward one of the rocks. There was a little Asian girl with straight black hair, and the blackest eyes that Donny had ever seen staring at him.

"...and our brother, Stephen..." continued Laura. On top of

another rock, a thin, curly-haired, red-headed boy glared at Donny.

"...and our sister, Keisha..." Jacob said. A little girl with African braids smiled wickedly at Donny from yet another rock.

The list seemed to go on forever: Billy, Ana, James, Lucia, Hector, Tiffany, Dylan. Every time they said a name, a new child would appear standing on top of another rock until it looked like a small army. There were approximately thirty children surrounding Donny. He felt afraid. He felt very afraid.

Donovan worked judiciously from his home office. It was a great way to earn a living. No clocking time, no commuting, no one breathing down your neck. He would drive into Manhattan about twice a month for meetings, but that was as close as he ever got to the dreaded rat race. He had just taken on a new project, and needed his best drawing implements, which he kept in a file cabinet by the window. He glanced out the window and looked at the beautiful view of the lake. He loved the water, but for some bizarre reason, it also made him nervous. It was like it reminded him of something that he could not quite remember. He pushed the thought from his mind and opened the drawer where his tools were. As he took them out, a small, blue envelope fell to the floor. Donovan put his implements aside and picked it up. It had his name on the front, and he held his breath for a moment when he recognized Susan's cursive handwriting. Donovan opened the envelope with shaky hands and read the note inside:

My Dearest Donny:

I am not writing this note to be cruel or melodramatic. I know how much you dislike that. I tried my absolute best to be a loving wife to you. I gave you all that nature would allow me to give. One of the most painful things for a woman to realize is that she will never be able to enjoy the blessing of motherhood. I can only hope that the woman you have chosen to replace me can make you happy by giving you what I could not.

Goodbye, Donny. I know that someday, you will make a great father.

Love always.

Susan

Donovan read the note over and over again until his head was spinning. He felt sweaty and nauseous, and just about ready to collapse. He tore the note to shreds, and darted out of the cabin like a madman, screaming, "Donny! Donny! Donny!"

He looked around wildly, and started running in short sprints, stopping every few feet and then changing direction. "Donny! Donny! Donny!"

The residents of the other cabins started coming out to see what all the commotion was about. Donovan bumped into Abe, the superintendent of the complex. "Hey there, where are you off to in such a rush?" Abe asked.

"I have to find Donny!" Donovan exclaimed.

Abe looked at him as if he were from another planet.

"Do you know where Donny is?" he grabbed Abe by the collar, shouting into his face.

"What's going on, Abe?" an elderly woman shouted out from her front porch.

"I don't know, Mrs. Scollan," Abe answered nervously. Donovan's hands were still on his collar. "I think Mr. Blake is having some sort of panic attack."

At first, Donovan did not understand anything. Then, suddenly, things became very clear in his mind. The last thing he thought before blacking out was *It can't be. That's impossible.*

Donovan had grown up in Lakeside before it became a luxury community. He had been raised by a single father who was also his namesake. To make the distinction between the two, everyone called the younger Blake, Donny. Mr. Blake worked at the local textile factory. He often worked double shifts, so Donny spent much of his childhood by himself. Mr. Blake was rarely able to drive his son to school, so he had to rely on the school bus. The driver was a pot-smoking, sixteen-year-old boy who went by the name of Snake. He was a kind of fifties version of Otto on The Simpsons, and he always walked as if though he were jamming to some funky tune that no one else could hear. Snake had a fourteen-year-old girlfriend named Crystal who looked twice his age. Rumor had it that before settling on Snake, she had already sampled most of the male population of Lakeside. She would often ride with Snake on the school bus. No one knew if she had any family, and no one seemed to care. Mr. Blake was never happy with this arrangement for his son's transportation, but his schedules at the factory left him little choice.

As it can probably be deduced, Snake was not the sharpest tool in the shed. He was generally high, and very easily distracted. Even though there were only about thirty children in Lakeside, he could never remember their names, nor did he really care to. When the children loaded the bus, he was usually smoking a joint, or feeling Crystal up behind the bus. When he first started the job, he attempted head counts, but the children would not stay still, and he was not a babysitter, so he stopped doing it all together.

Due to Snake's limited attention span, it was extremely easy to ditch school, and some of the children did it often. Among them were Donny and his two best friends, Jacob and Laura. They spent most days by the lake, and an extraordinarily strong bond grew between them. Jacob, being the oldest, was their leader. He was wild and adventurous, and considered himself quite the explorer. Laura was a very adventurous girl as well, but Donny could not help seeing her as a goddess. He was completely taken in by her wavy, blonde hair, and long eyelashes. Donny planned to ask her to marry him when they grew up. Even though she was an older woman, a full year his senior, Donny was willing to put their age difference aside, and make her his wife.

One day, a field trip had been organized by the school, and since this was such a rare occurrence, all the children were eagerly waiting outside when the bus arrived that morning. Snake and Crystal had attended a wild party the night before and were still feeling the effects of all the substances floating around in their systems.

"Wow, babe. Where did all these little runts come from?" Snake asked in a daze.

"Yeah, it's like a creepy kid invasion," Crystal answered from beyond the mist of her own clouded mind.

The carnival that the children were going to was three towns away, so it would be quite a long trip. Jacob, Laura, and Donny had decided that it would be fun to play a joke on everyone and fake a series of explosions. They had been able to get together a few cherry bombs and planned to set them off inside the bus. They were harmless enough, but it would give everyone a good scare.

A few minutes before the bus was about to leave, Laura jumped up in her seat. "The matches!"

"Shit!" Jacob said, and the three children started searching their pockets frantically.

"I've got two!" Laura said triumphantly.

"That's not enough," Donny said. "We have six cherry bombs."

"I guess we can only set two off," Jacob said with disappointment in his voice.

Donny felt bad but was ready for resignation until he looked over at Laura. In her face there was an expression beyond disappointment. It was sadness. Donny could not allow his future wife to be sad. His face lit up as he said, "My father has matches in his desk."

"Forget it," Jacob said. "We don't have time. The bus is already loaded, and we'll be leaving any minute."

Donny looked out the window, and saw Snake and Crystal brazenly groping each other. It did not seem like they would be stopping any time soon.

"Snake is making out with Crystal. I can make it home, and back again before they even realize I'm gone."

"I wouldn't mind making out with Crystal. She is hot stuff!" Jacob said.

Laura looked at Jacob with disgust, and turned to Donny with big, hopeful eyes. "Do you think you're fast enough, Donny?"

The wonder and adoration in Laura's eyes were enough incentive for Donny. He would not only secure the success of the prank they had planned, but he would also be a hero in Laura's eyes. This was an opportunity he could not pass up. Donny dashed off the bus and ran to the cabin as fast as his little legs could carry him, ignoring Jacob's insistence that there was not enough time. All he could think about was completing the mission and impressing Laura. As soon as Donny was out of sight, Snake and Crystal walked onto the bus. Snake started the engine and closed the door. Crystal turned over a milk crate and sat next to him. They paid no attention to Jacob and Laura's pleas to wait for Donny.

"If you snooze, you lose," Crystal said nonchalantly, and the bus took off.

Even though Donny had found the matches right away, when he ran back outside, he could only see a yellow blur in the distance. He had not accomplished his mission. Donny was heartbroken. He would never be a hero to Laura now.

On the bus, the children were as rowdy as expected, and Snake and Crystal could not keep their hands off each other. Every now and then, the bus would swerve when they got too hot and heavy, but the children did not seem to mind. In fact, they rather enjoyed it, and squealed in delight. It added further adventure to their field trip. At one point, Crystal started unzipping Snake's jeans. Snake stiffened in the driver's seat. "Not here, babe. The kids." Even in his intoxicated state, he realized that this was beyond inappropriate.

"Come on, Snake," Crystal purred at him. "Let Crystal play with your BIG snake."

As much as Snake wanted to just stop the bus and let Crystal have her way, he did not want to get fired. He knew that he was not that bright, and that it would be hard for him to find employment elsewhere. He roughly slapped her hand off, while keeping one hand on the wheel. With his free hand, he zipped up his jeans again. Crystal was obviously not used to being rejected, especially by some dim-witted teenage boy. She stood up angrily and yelled at him. "Is your brain so fried that you can't get it up, or did you suddenly become a faggot?"

"You're such a slut!" he screamed back at her.

Meanwhile, the children on the bus had already begun

roughhousing, and papers and food were flying every which way. Everyone was distracted. It was the perfect time for Jacob and Laura to put their plan into action. It was a shame that Donny was not with them. It had been his idea after all. Each one of them took a cherry bomb and lit it simultaneously. Then they let them roll toward the front of the bus.

They went off within seconds of each other next to Crystal's feet. She shrieked hysterically, and roughly grabbed hold of Snake's arm, claiming that that her leg was burning. This made Snake lose control of the wheel, and the bus started swerving wildly. Most of the children were out of their seats and started painfully knocking against one another.

Lakeside was a community built around the lake. No matter what direction you went, the lake was close by. No one had ever bothered to build guardrails along the side of the road that would separate it from the great body of water. The land formations also became higher as you got further away from Lakeside. By the time the bus lost control its elevation was high, and the fall was steep. The bus went off the road, and straight into the lake. There were no survivors. The passengers never even had a chance. Weeks later, individual autopsies would show that very few of the victims had died on impact. Most of them had to spend their last moments on earth desperately trying to escape their vehicular prison while their lungs filled with water, and their eyes bulged out of their sockets.

It took a long time for Donny to accept what had happened. At first, he simply refused to believe that his friends and classmates were gone. Then, the survivor's guilt settled in, and it became worse. He was supposed to be with them that day. He had abandoned his friends, and that was the only reason he was still alive. He started having recurring nightmares about dead children pulling him into the lake with their decaying hands, and unearthly moans. The worst was one where Laura kept trying to kiss him. She would open her puffy blue lips and expose a horrible picture of mangled gums and rotted teeth. She would then stick out a black tongue and speak. "Don't you want to kiss me, Donny? I thought you were in love with me."

Donovan came to with a violent shudder, and saw himself surrounded by his Lakeside Gardens neighbors, frightened faces mingled with those of genuine concern. Others showed clear signs of morbid curiosity, and still others, slight traces of amusement.

"Are you all right, Mr. Blake?" Abe asked, his wrinkled face at kissing distance from Donovan's.

"I'm fine," Donovan answered, gently pushing Abe away. "I just had a bad dream." He stood up and brushed himself off. He turned to his neighbors. "I'm sorry I frightened everyone."

"Are you sure you don't want me to call a doctor? He can probably make it here pretty quickly," Abe offered.

"That won't be necessary," Donovan answered. "I just need to go in and rest." He turned toward his cabin and started walking away. He then made a half-turn toward Abe and thanked him. The small crowd that had formed started to dissolve as it realized that the show was over. There was nothing more to see.

As he looked at the almost motionless water of the lake, Donovan thought to himself, *The calm before the storm*. Once again, the small voice behind him asked, "Is it time yet?" This time Donovan did not turn around. There was nothing to see. He had told Abe and his other neighbors that he had had a bad dream. To a certain extent, this was the truth. He now realized that most of his life had been a dream. How could he have forgotten about his childhood in Lakeside? It was obviously not a coincidence that he would end up here again almost fifty years later. Destiny had brought him back. He had hidden his demons so well that he had almost convinced himself that they were never there. Almost. Now it was time to face them. Everything had come around full circle. "It's time," he said aloud and stared out at the lake.

The night sky had already covered Lakeside Gardens. The water in the lake started bubbling as if it were a humungous witch's cauldron, gently at first, and then viciously. Small shadows emerged from the lake producing eerie sounds that formed a horribly strident demonic melody. Donovan watched in horror as his schoolmates from half a century ago materialized before his eyes. Their features were recognizable enough, but their bodies were in advanced states of decay. They came toward Donovan with slow, jerky movements that made his blood turn to ice. He remembered every one of them. Snake and Crystal were also there. They licked and caressed each other's bodies ravenously. Even after fifty years of death, they had not learned to control themselves.

Donovan felt his heartbeat accelerate at an incredible pace. It became difficult for him to breathe, and all that would come out were intercut, wheezy gasps. He felt his muscles begin to spasm violently, and he cried out in pain, but it was not his own voice. It was that of a terrified eight-year-old boy. His frame began to shrink, and his skin became soft and flawless as it had been so many years ago. His thinning hair flourished with the strength and dark color that had characterized his boyhood. When the transformation was complete, Donny started shivering like a frightened mouse awaiting a cat's killer pounce. He closed his eyed firmly and screamed when he felt arms on him.

"What's wrong, Donny?" a sweet, familiar voice asked him.

Donny looked up timidly and saw Laura's beautiful,

princess-like visage staring down at him. Her warm glow relaxed him immediately, and he realized that it was no longer nighttime. He was no longer in Lakeside Gardens. He was in the Lakeside of his childhood, no fancy complex, no affluent retirees, just the dusty town he grew up in. It was a beautiful, sunny day, and he was near the lake with his friend, Laura.

"Come on," Laura urged him. "Everyone's at the lake." She took his hand and led him to the lake.

When they got there, it was the most joyous sight Donny had ever seen. Children were chasing each other and laughing. Some were swimming. Others were playfully splashing one another. Jacob waved at them from the top of a rock and did a belly flop into the water as the children giggled in delight. Snake and Crystal were there holding hands, but Donny had never seen them like this before. They were clean and well-groomed, and they hugged and kissed each other with genuine affection. It was beautiful.

As Crystal saw Donny and Laura approaching, she called out, "OK, kids. The gang's all here. Everybody in the water!"

At her command, everyone who was not in the lake rushed in. Donny and Laura followed suit and dove in with a splash. Once they were all in the water, Snake said "OK. Now let's see who can hold his breath the longest!"

With the discipline of a military platoon, everyone went underwater immediately. Only Donny and Laura remained above the surface. Laura hugged him close and said, "Don't be afraid, Donny. We're together now."

They both went under. Donny took a deep breath of air and felt ecstatic in Laura's arms. He felt he could remain like this forever, but obviously, he could not. When he felt the need for air, he freed himself from Laura's embrace, and went above the surface to find that it was nighttime again, and he was alone. From where he was, he could see the lights of the Lakeside Gardens cabins.

"Laura?" he called out, but there was no answer. "Jacob?"

The lake started bubbling again, and Donny felt fear take hold of his heart once again. The rotted corpses of the children started surfacing from the water, and swimming toward him. Donny started screaming hysterically, but more and more children converged upon him. Small arms were pulling at him from every direction as he helplessly struggled to free himself. Suddenly, Laura came out from the water, but it was not his beloved, childhood friend. It was the horrid thing from his nightmares.

"Now we can be together forever!" she moaned in a voice that chilled Donny to the bone.

She pounced on him, and with the aid of the other children, pulled him down to the cold and dark bottom of the lake.

Abe stood inside Donovan's cabin talking to a police officer. He did not try to hide his face of disbelief at the situation.

"Thank you very much for your help," the officer said. "We may need to contact you at a later time."

Abe nodded his head slowly. "What happened?"

"It appears that Mr. Blake may have suffered a heart attack while in the bathtub." The officer scratched his head. "But it doesn't quite add up."

"What doesn't add up?" Abe inquired.

"Well, first, he is still dressed, and there isn't much water in the tub to begin with. Also, the medical examiner says that due to the condition of the body, and the position that we found it in, the cause of death is most probably drowning.'

"Drowning?" Abe exclaimed. "In a bathtub?"

"We won't know for sure until the autopsy is done, but it certainly looks that way."

Behind the two men, the bathroom door was wide open. Donovan Blake, fully clothed and face down, was inside the bathtub. His body was bloated, and he floated grotesquely in a shallow pool of stagnant water. Later that morning, when the body was finally moved, Donovan's facial expression would be seen, forever frozen in a grimace of pain and terror.

CPSIA information can be obtained
at www.ICGtesting.com
Printed in the USA
LVHW051732220723
753118LV00002B/185

9 781800 746381